UNITED KINGDOM

Regent's Park內的運河

Regent's
Canal

London Zoo

Regent's Park

Hyde Park

Buckingham Pala

海德公園(Hyde Park）一角

白金漢宮(Buckingham Palace)和衛兵的換班

西敏寺(Westminster Abbey)

大英博物館

特拉法加廣場 (Trafalgar Square)

彼加得利廣場 (Piccadilly Square)

ON

dilly
s

●Trafalgar
Square

River Thames

Houses of Parliament

Westminster
Abbey

泰晤士河 (the Thames) 和國會 (Houses of Parliament)

LEARNER'S
ALL TALKS 2

LEARNING PUBLISHING CO., LTD.

ALL TALKS

PRINTED IN TAIWAN

supervisor   :   Samuel Liu
text design   :   Jessica Y.P. Chen
illustrations   :   Vivian Wang, Amanda Chang
cover design   :   Isabella Chang

ACKNOWLEDGEMENTS

We would like to thank all the people whose ongoing support has made this project so enjoyable and rewarding. At the top of the list of those who provided insight, inspiration, and helpful suggestions for revisions are:

David Bell
Pei-ting Lin
Cherry Cheing
Nick Veitch
Joanne Beckett
Thomas Deneau
Stacy Schultz
David M. Quesenberry
Kirk Kofford
Francesca A. Evans
Jeffrey R. Carr
Chris Virani

序　言

　　編者在受教育的過程中，常覺國內的英語教育，欠缺一套好的會話教材。根據我們最近所做的研究顯示，各級學校的英語老師與關心的讀者也都深深覺得，我們用的進口會話教材，版面密密麻麻，不但引不起學習興趣，所學又不盡與實際生活相關。像一般會話書上所教的早餐，總是教外國人吃的 *cereal*（麥片粥），而完全沒有提及中國人早餐吃的**稀飯**（香港餐館一般翻成 " *congee* "，美國人叫 " *rice soup* "）、豆漿（ *soy bean milk* ）、燒餅（ *baked roll* ）、油條（ *Chinese fritter* ）該如何適切地表達？

　　我們有感於一套好的教材必須能夠真正引發學生的興趣，內容要切合此時此地（ *here and now* ）及讀者確實的需求，也就是要本土化、具體化。

　　五年多來，在這種共識之下，我們全體編輯群秉持專業化的精神，實地蒐集、調查日常生活中天天用得到、聽得到的會話，加以歸類、整理，並設計生動有趣的教學活動，彙編成「ＡＴ美語會話教本」這套最適合中國人的會話教材。

　　這套教材不僅在資料蒐集上力求完美，而且從構思到成書，都投入極大的心力。在編纂期間，特別延聘國內外教學權威，利用這套教材開班授課，由本公司全體編輯當學生，在學習出版門市部親自試用，以求發掘問題，加以修正。因此，這套教材的每一課都經過不斷的實驗改進，每一頁都經過不斷地字斟句酌，輸入中國人的智慧。

　　經由我們的示範教學證明這套教材，祇要徹底弄懂，受過嚴格要求者，英語會話能力定能突飛猛進，短時間內達到高效果。這套教材在編審的每個階段，都務求審慎，唯仍恐有疏失之處，敬祈各界先進不吝指正。

編者　謹識

AT 美語會話教本

課程簡介

AT美語 會話教本	程度	適　用　對　象	備　註
ALL TALKS ①②	初級	1. 具備國中英語程度、初學英會話的讀者。 2. 適合高中、高職、五專的初級英會課程。	已出版
AMERICAN TALKS ①②	中級	1. 具備高中英語程度，以前學過英會的讀者。 2. 適合高中、高職、五專的進階英會課程。 3. 大專程度的初級課程。	已出版
ADVANCED TALKS ①②	高級	1. 想進一步充實流利口語，言之有物的讀者。 2. 大專程度進階用。	已出版

　　全套教材分初、中、高三級；每級二冊，全套共六冊。每冊皆根據教育部頒定的「英語會話課程標準」而設計，每冊十四課。因此可配合各校授課的學年長短，作各種不同的組合利用：

(1) 一學年（兩學期）：採用初級教本 ALL TALKS①②，內容包括基礎生活會話及一般常見的實用口語，讓同學們學會用最簡單的英語來溝通，打好會話的基礎。

(2) 二學年（四學期）：採用中級教本 AMERICAN TALKS①② 及高級教本 ADVANCED TALKS①②。這四冊的內容、人物均可連貫，自成系統。程度由淺入深，舉凡一般簡單的問候、招呼語到基礎商用、談論時事、宗教等會話皆包括在內，涵蓋面廣，可讓同學們循序漸進地培養實力。

(3) 三學年（六學期）：採用全套「AT美語會話教本」六冊，利用一系列設計的整套內容，經由螺旋式教學法，也就是在第一學年教完 ALL TALKS，讓同學們稍具基礎之後，第二、三學年再接著教授 AMERICAN TALKS 及 ADVAN-CED TALKS；一面將前面學過的內容加以整合，一面適度地添加程度與課程，幫助同學們溫故知新，兼顧語言使用的正確性與流暢性。

CONTENTS

CHARACTERS

Lesson 1 I Lost My Wallet

Listen and repeat
after your teacher.

(A) LET'S TALK

A : I lost my wallet.

B : What's your name, please?

A : Bob Young.

B : Could you describe the wallet for me?

A : Sure — it's brown leather, about so big.

B : How much did you have inside?

A : About fifty dollars. Plus my driver's license and
all my credit cards.

B : And where were you when you first noticed it missing?

A : Right over there.

B : Okay, we'll let you know if it turns up.

🔊 (B) LET'S PRACTICE

Learn the following phrases and do the practice with your partner.

(1) Lost Items

1. I've lost my suitcase.
2. I've had my wallet stolen.
3. I had my purse stolen.
4. I had my wallet stolen with my passport.
5. I have lost my passport somewhere.
6. I'm afraid I've lost my traveler's checks.

(2) Asking for Further Details

7. Could you describe the wallet for me?
8. What kind of wallet is it?
9. How much did you have inside?
10. Where were you when you first noticed it missing?
11. What's in your suitcase?
12. Where did you buy those traveller's checks?
13. Did you check the lost and found?
14. When did you first miss your suitcase?

(3) More Descriptions

15. It's brown leather, about so big.
16. It's black with a gold pin.
17. About 100 dollars. Plus my passport and all my credit cards.

18. I'm not sure where I left it.

19. It has everything in it.

20. I purchased them at the American Express office in Taipei.

PRACTICE 1

Work in pairs. Take turns playing a policeman and a person who had something stolen. Practice describing the loss to the police.

1. You've lost a wallet. Pick any three items to be in your wallet.

2. Take out your own wallet or purse. Suppose you just had it stolen on the bus. Try to describe it to the policeman.

(4) **Yelling for Help**

21. Thief !

22. Burglar !

23. Fire !

24. Pickpocket !

25. Murder !

26. Shoplifter !

27. Police !

28. Ambulance !

29. Help me !

30. This is an emergency.

(5) Notifying the Police

31. Call the police right away, please.

32. Where is the police station?

33. Should I go to the police station?

34. I'd like to notify the police immediately.

35. Please make the report so I can make a damage claim to my insurance company.

36. We'll let you know if it turns up.

PRACTICE 2

Work in groups of 3 or 4. Discuss what to do if one of the following things happened.

LESSON 1

🎧 (C) LET'S PLAY

● For Student A

Learn the following sentence patterns first, and ask your partner for the information you need.

Is	this a bank? he pulling something?		That's right. Not exactly.	
Are	they in the living room? they watching TV?		No,	he is not. they're not.

Is	there	a man a dog	in the other picture?	Yes, there	is. are.
		family mem- bers		No, there	is not. are not.

I think Maybe	he is they are	pulling a wagon in the street. watching a TV news program.

● Work in pairs. Try to guess what is happening in the other half of the picture. You have 3 chances to guess each picture.

1.

2.

3.

4.

5.

6.

LESSON 1

🎧 (C) LET'S PLAY

● For Student B

Learn the following sentence patterns first, and ask your partner for the information you need.

Is	this a bank ? he pulling something ?
Are	they in the living room ? they watching TV ?

That's right. Not exactly.	
No,	he is not. they're not.

Is	there	a man a dog	in the other picture ?
Are		family mem- bers	

Yes, there	is. are.
No, there	is not. are not.

I think Maybe	he is they are	pulling a wagon in the street. watching a TV news program.

● **Work in pairs. Try to guess what is happening in the other half of the picture. You have 3 chances to guess each picture.**

1.　　　　　　　　2.　　　　　　　　3.

4.　　　　　　　　5.　　　　　　　　6.

LESSON 1

Exercise

Complete the following dialogue and make your own conversation.

(1) **Dialogue**

A : I had my wallet _____ .

B : Where were you when you first noticed it _____ .

A : On the third floor.

B : Can you _____ the wallet for me ?

A : Yes, it's black _____ a gold pin.

B : Did you check the _____ and _____ ?

A : Not yet.

B : Let's see if it might have turned _____ .

(2) **Cartoon**

Lesson 2   Are You Free This Weekend?

Listen and repeat after your teacher.

(A) LET'S TALK

A : Why don't we go out together sometime?

B : I'd love to. When would you like to go out?

A : Are you free this weekend?

B : Well, I have classes on Friday, but I'm free after that.

A : Great! Then what would you say to dinner and a movie?

B : Sounds nice. What movie do you want to see?

A : Do you like horror movies?

B : Yuck! How about a comedy or something?

A : All right. Shall I pick you up at seven?

B : It's a date!

LESSON 2

(B) LET'S PRACTICE

Learn the following phrases and do the practice with your partner.

(1) **Asking For an Appointment**

1. When would be most convenient for you ?
2. When shall we make it ?
3. When can you make it ?
4. When will it be convenient for you to visit me ?
5. What time could I come and see him ?
6. What time can I come and see the manager ?
7. May I see you tomorrow ?
8. Will you be free this afternoon ?
9. Is 3 o'clock convenient for you ?
10. Would two-thirty suit you ?
11. How about next Wednesday afternoon at 2 o'clock ?
12. Is 4 o'clock all right with you ?

(2) **Setting the Time and Place**

13. Let's meet in the lobby of the Hilton Hotel at 2:30 tomorrow afternoon.
14. Any time will suit me.
15. Any time will be convenient for me.
16. That'll suit me perfectly.
17. I'll be expecting you around two.
18. I'll be there between two and two-thirty.

PRACTICE 1

Work in pairs. Write down your own schedule for the week. Then agree on a time when both of you can get together. If you say yes, be sure to agree on the details below. If you say no, think of a suitable excuse.

---

1. Is it a date? Or just a friendly outing?
2. Where will you meet? At what time?
3. Where will you go? What will you do?

	Mon	Tue	Wed	Thr	Fri	Sat	Sun
A.M.							
P.M.							

---

(3) **Meeting with Someone**

19. I don't have an appointment, but this is rather urgent.
20. I'd like to make an appointment now.
21. Could you spare me a few minutes?
22. May I have a few minutes with you?
23. I'd like to see Mr. Wilson, please.
24. I have an appointment with Mr. Wilson at 3 o'clock.
25. I wonder if I could see Mr. Wilson.
26. May I see John for just a moment?
27. I have a letter of introduction to Mr. Wilson from Mr. Lee.
28. I phoned earlier for an appointment.

PRACTICE 2

Work in pairs. Practice making appointments with your partner according to the situations below. Then switch roles.

1. come to my office to discuss the plan

2. go to the movies together

3. visit me

4. meet Mr. Wilson with a previous appointment

5. meet the manager without an appointment

6. meet the president with a letter of introduction

LESSON 2

🎧 **(C) LET'S PLAY**   ● For Student AB

Learn the following sentence patterns first, and do the activity with your partner.

Since	he she	was a field manager, studied computer science, has an MBA,

	he she	ought to can will be able to	skip training. manage well.

Claire Frederick Skip	would make a good	salesperson manager

because	she has experience. she can speak French. he is young.

If we hire	Bill, Sarah, Frederick,	then we	can't won't be able to have to	hire take	Claire. Bill. Skip.

His Her	education experience skills	will	come in handy. meet our needs.

● **For the Teacher**

Let students work in pairs. They are members of a recruiting committee. They have interviewed six candidates for two jobs. Here are the candidates, along with short resumés and expected annual salaries (in U.S. dollars) !

$45,000

Bill Robertson

B.A. (*Accounting*)
MBA (*Finance*)

Six years experience
as a loan officer
in a bank

$35,000

Sarah Wulf

B.A. (*French*)

Assistant manager
of a small retail
shop for four years

$ 25.000

Angela Harris

B.A. (*Chemistry*)

Field manager for African relief project for 1½ years.

$ 20.000

Skip Crone

B.A. (*Music*)

No full-time work experience. Serves weekends in the City Hall.

$ 30.000

Frederick Pohl

B.A., M.A., Ph.D. (*History*)

Thirteen years' teaching experience at the university level.

$ 22.000

Claire Wyneckie

B.A. (*Computer Science*)

Three years experience as a secretary.

● **You have budgeted $ 65,000 to fill the two positions described below. Discuss with your partner and make a final decision.**

Branch manager

Responsible for supervising a staff of 30, submitting an operating budget, selecting suppliers and distributors, coordinating a marketing plan

Salesperson

Should be capable of representing the company's product to potential distributors, after a brief period of technical training

● Which two candidates would you hire ? Why ?

LESSON 2

Exercise

Complete the following dialogues and make your own conversation.

(1) **Dialogue**

A : We must _____ sometime next week.
B : OK. When can you _____?

A : _____ Friday afternoon ?
B : Hmm ... _____ .

A : Good. Do you want to meet _____ ?
B : Sure. No problem.

      *   *   *   *

A : Can I help you ?
B : Yes. I'd like _____ .

A : Do you have _____ ?
B : Yes. I _____ this morning. He wanted me to drop by.

A : Give me your name, please. I'll tell him you're here.

(2) **Cartoon**

Lesson 3  May I Speak to Mr. Davis?

Listen and repeat after your teacher.

(A) LET'S TALK

A : Hello, Tower Corporation.
B : Hello, this is Lisa Welch. May I speak to Mr. Davis ?

A : I'm sorry, but Mr. Davis is out of the office.
B : Do you know when he'll be back ?

A : Maybe later today. May I take a message ?
B : Okay. Just tell him that Lisa Welch called...

A : Is that "Welch" with a W-E-L-C-H ?
B : Right. And ask him to call me back.

A : Got it. Does Mr. Davis have your number ?
B : Let me give it to you just in case. It's 743...

A : Wait a moment — he just came in. Mr. Davis ! Line 2 !

LESSON 3

● (B) LET'S PRACTICE

Learn the following phrases and do the practice with your partner.

(1) Placing a Call

1. May I speak to Mr. Smith ?
2. Is this Mr. White's residence ?
3. Is Jenny at home ?
4. Is my husband in ?
5. Could you connect me with Mr. Brown ?
6. Will you put me through to the production department ?
7. Extension 166, please.
8. Could I speak to Helen, please ?

(2) Picking up the Receiver

9. Who is calling?
10. Hello, this is she.
11. This is David Lee speaking.

(3) Problems

12. I'm afraid you have the wrong number.
13. I'm sorry. I've called the wrong number.
14. What number are you calling ?
15. We were cut off.
16. I can't get through.
17. The lines seem to be crossed.

18. There's no one by that name here.

19. Please hang up the receiver and dial again.

PRACTICE 1

Work in pairs. Take turns making and answering a call. Use the situations below.

1. John Wood is making a call to Mr. Brown's residence, and Mr. Brown takes the receiver.

2. Mr. Smith wants to speak to Mr. Johnson in the Sales Department, and the operator tells him to dial extension 178.

3. David Lee would like to speak to Jenny White, but has the wrong number.

4. The line is cut off. The operator tells you to hang up and dial again.

(4) **The Person Is Not In**

20. He is not at his desk at the moment.

21. I'm sorry. He is out at the moment.

22. When do you expect him back?

23. I'll call again later.

24. I think he'll be back in about an hour.

(5) **Taking a Message**

25. Shall I take a message?

26. May I leave a message for him?

27. Shall I have him call you back?

28. Would you tell him that I called?

29. Could you ask him to call me at 713-5678?

30. Would you please ask him to call back?

31. Certainly. May I have your phone number?

(6) **Tranferring the Call**

32. Please hold on.

33. Hold on a minute, please.

34. One moment, please.

35. Just a moment, sir.

36. You're wanted on the phone.

37. There's a phone call for you from Mr. Carter.

38. The line is busy.

39. He is on another phone now. Would you like to wait?

40. Mr. Morgan is on the line.

PRACTICE 2

Work in pairs. One of you play a businessman who telephones a client. The other is the client's secretary. Use the following situations as a guide.

1. The businessman has urgent news, but the client is very busy and doesn't want to be disturbed.

2. The message is urgent, but the client is out of the office.

3. The client is in another part of the building. (Transfer the call)

LESSON 3

🎧 (C) LET'S PLAY

●For the Whole Class

Learn the following sentence patterns first, and do the activity with your classmates.

He said She told him	(that)	the car wouldn't start.		
He asked if		she was going to have a baby.		

The boy	told	the girl	to shine his shoes.	
The secretary		the client	that the boss was away.	

The clerk	asked	the boss	for a promotion.	
The man		the politician	not to raise taxes.	

Indirect Quotations

● Look at the pictures on the next page for 2 minutes. Then cover them up. Test your memory by seeing how many questions you can answer.

Example: ☆ The lazy man said that he hated mornings.

☆ The motorcycle driver told the old lady to

_____ .

☆ The politician promised _____ .

☆ The little boy told his dog to _____ .

☆ _____ told her husband_____ .

☆ _____ asked his boss for a _____ .

☆ _____ said his car _____ .

☆ The secretary said _____ .

☆ _____ told the soldier that _____ .

☆ The little girl gave _____ .

☆ The little boy said _____ .

☆ The student said _____ .

☆ The workman asked _____ .

I hate mornings.

7:00

LESSON 3

Exercise

Complete the following dialogue and make your own conversation.

(1) Dialogues

- A : Is my husband _____?
  B : I'm sorry, he _____ .

  A : When _____ ?
  B : _____ three o'clock, I think.

- A : Hello, _____ Miss Chang ?
  B : She'll be _____ with you.

- A : I'd like to _____ , please.
  B : I'll _____ him for you.

- A : ABC's Laundry Service.
  B : I'm sorry. I called _____ .

- A : Is Mr. Smith in ?
  B : There is no one here _____ that name. What number _____ ?

(2) Cartoon

Lesson 4 I'd Like to Make a Collect Call

**Listen and repeat
after your teacher.**

🎧 (A) LET'S TALK

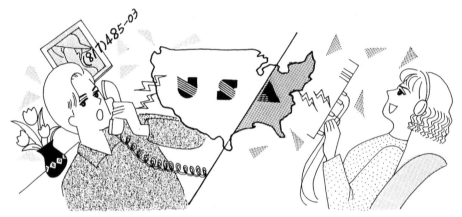

A : Operator. May I help you ?

B : I'd like to make a collect call to the United States, please.

A : What number, please ?

B : Area code (817) 485-0306.

A : And your name ?

B : John.

A : Hold on, please. (*The phone rings.*)

C : Hello ?

A : You have a collect call from John. Will you accept the charges ?

C : Yes, I will.

A : Your party is on the line. Please go ahead.

LESSON 4

(B) LET'S PRACTICE

Learn the following phrases and do the practice with your partner.

(1) Calling Overseas

1. I'd like to make an international call to Tokyo.
2. I'd like to make a long-distance call to Chicago.
3. I'd like to make a person-to-person call to Mr. Harold Davis.
4. Please make it a person-to-person call.
5. Will you please connect me with the overseas operator?
6. Overseas call, please.
7. Make it a collect call, please.
8. I'd like to make a collect call to Taipei, Taiwan.
9. A collect call, please.
10. Station-to-station call, please.
11. My party's name is David Lee.
12. The area code is 107, and the telephone number is 366-4871.
13. Please cancel that call.
14. I'd like to place a call to London.

(2) Instructions from the Operator

15. What kind of call are you going to make?
16. Will this be a person to person call?
17. What number, please?
18. May I have the telephone number?

19. Would you tell me the number in Japan?

20. And your name?

21. Are you going to pay for the call?

22. Hang up and wait, please.

23. Hold on, please.

24. Hold on a minute.

25. Hold the line, please.

26. I'll call you back later.

27. Your party is on the line.

28. Please go ahead.

PRACTICE 1

Work in pairs. One of you is the operator; the other wants to make a call.

1. You need to call home long-distance, but you don't have enough money.

2. You want to call your office in Dallas. You don't care who answers.

3. You want to speak to Paul Wilson personally in San Francisco.

(3) **Directory Assistance**

29. Could you tell me the area code for St. Louis?

30. I'd like to know the phone number of Peabody Hotel.

31. Could you give me the number of the Hilton Hotel?

32. What's the city code for Paris?

33. Operator, get me the police.

34. Operator, I need an ambulance.

35. Operator, please get me the fire department.

PRACTICE 2

Work in pairs. One of you is the operator; the other wants to make a call.

1. You want to give a call to Miss Fiona Lee, who stays in room 102, Green Hotel now. But you don't know the number of Green Hotel.

2. You'd like to place an overseas call to Paris. But you don't know the city code.

3. You are walking along Wilson Avenue. There is a building on fire and some persons are injured. Hurry to call for an ambulance and the fire department.

(4) **Long-Distance Charges**

36. You have a collect call from Mr. Davis in Chicago. Will you accept the charges ?

37. Will you please tell me the length of the call and charge later ?

38. I'd like to know the charge now.

39. How much was the call ?

40. Please charge it to my room.

PRACTICE 3

Work in pairs. Take turns playing the operator and the person who wants to make a call.

You want to place an overseas call from the hotel. ⇨

Try to connect with the overseas operator through the front desk. ⇨

Make it a person-to person call.

Give your name, your party's name and the telephone number (with area code) to the operator. ⇨

The operator will find out if the party can answer the call. ⇨

Finally, you want to know the charge and the length of the call.

LESSON 4

🎧 (C) LET'S PLAY

● For Student A

Learn the following sentence patterns first, and ask your partner for the information you need.

Excuse me, I want to ..... What do I have to do?
OK. Then what?
I see. What's next?
Is that all?
Oh, I see. Thanks.

Well, first ......
Then, you have to ......
Next you ......
Well, finally you have to ......

● **Ask your partner how to**

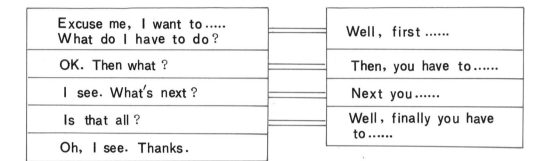

(1) Get a driver's license　(2) Wash the clothes

● **Here are clues for teaching your partner how to**

(1) Take out some money

(2) Scramble some eggs

LESSON 4

🎧 (C) LET'S PLAY

● For Student B

Learn the following sentence patterns first, and ask your partner for the information you need.

Excuse me, I want to ...... What do I have to do?	Well, first ......
OK. Then what?	Then, you have to ......
I see. What's next?	Next you ......
Is that all?	Well, finally you have to ......
Oh, I see. Thanks.	

● **Ask your partner how to**

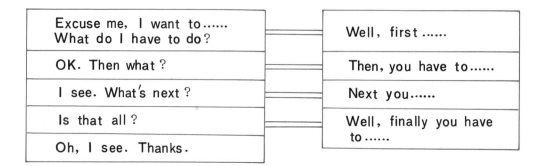

(1) Take out some money

(2) Scramble some eggs

● **Here are clues for teaching your partner how to**

(1) Get a driver's license

(2) Wash the clothes

LESSON 4

Exercise

Complete the following dialogue and make your own conversation.

(1) **Dialogue**

A : Operator, may I＿＿＿＿＿you ?

B : I'd like to place a ＿＿＿＿＿to London.

A : What＿＿＿＿＿＿, please ?

B : Country code 44, area＿＿＿＿＿1, 640097.

A : Will this be a ＿＿＿＿＿ to ＿＿＿＿＿ call ?

B : No, ＿＿＿＿＿ it a station call.

A : Your party is on the＿＿＿＿＿ now.

B : Hello, operator ? We have a bad ＿＿＿＿＿＿＿ . I can't hear a thing.

A : Please＿＿＿＿＿ on.

(2) **Cartoon**

Lesson 5 I'd Love to Come

Listen and repeat after your teacher.

🎧 (A) LET'S TALK

A : Do you have any plans for tomorrow evening?
Say around six?

B : Not yet. Why do you ask?

A : My parents would like to have you over for dinner.

B : Thanks — I'd love to come!

A : They're looking forward to meeting you.

B : It was really nice of them to invite me.

A : Do you like Italian food?

B : Sounds delicious. Can I bring anything?

A : Just your appetite.

B : In that case, I'll see you tomorrow at six!

LESSON 5

Learn the following phrases and do the practice with your partner.

(1) Issuing an Invitation

1. I'd like to invite you to my house.
2. I'd like to invite you to dinner.
3. Could you come to dinner?
4. I would like to have you over for dinner.
5. Let me treat you to dinner.
6. Please be my guest.
7. Would you like to join us for lunch?
8. We would like to invite you to dinner next Sunday.
9. We'd like to invite you to dinner sometime next week.
10. I wonder if you and your wife would be able to come to a party.
11. Why don't you come to a party at my place?

(2) Accepting an Invitation

12. Thanks, I'd love to come.
13. Yes, with pleasure.
14. I accept your invitation with pleasure.
15. Thank you for inviting me. I'm sure I can come.
16. Yes, I'd love to, but where exactly?
17. Sure. I'd like to.
18. Thank you. I'll be very happy to come.
19. That's great. I'd be pleased to.
20. Oh, we'd very much like to. Thank you for inviting us.

PRACTICE I

Work in pairs. Take turns issuing and accepting invitations. Use the information below.

1. over for dinner

2. nice restaurant

3. rock concert

4. symphony

5. art museum

6. birthday party

7. dancing party

8. picnic

9. graduation ceremony

(3) Declining an Invitation

21. I'd really like to, but I just can't, I'm afraid.

22. It's nice of you to ask, but I won't be able to come.

23. Thanks all the same.

24. It's very kind of you to invite me, but I'm sorry I can't come.

25. I'd like to, but I'm afraid I can't make it this time.

26. I wish I could, but I have something to do today.

27. I have another engagement on that day.

28. I have a previous engagement.

(4) Suggesting an Alternative Time

29. Can't you make it another day?

30. What about Friday?

31. Can we change it to another day?

32. Let's make it some other time.

33. Please ask me again some other time.

PRACTICE 2

Work in pairs. Take turns declining the invitations either with an excuse or by suggesting an alternative time. Use the situations in PRACTICE 1.

LESSON 5

🎧 (C) LET'S PLAY

● For Student A

Learn the following sentence patterns first, and ask your partner for the information you need.

Does	it this dish	contain have	any very much a lot of	salt meat ? fat

Do	you they	have any	low-calorie vegetarian	dishes ?

What	is chili made of ?
	is in the lasagna ?

Do you	like prefer	spicy food ? meat ? dairy products?
Can you eat		

STEP 1 You'd like to invite your partner out for dinner. Tell him about your favorite restaurant.

Giovanni's
Café Italiano!

Spaghetti
    with meat balls
    with meat sauce ·················· 170 NT
Pizza   toppings: mushrooms, Canadian bacon, chives, green
    peppers, extra cheese. ················· 280 NT
Ravioli   (small dumplings filled with meat or cheese and
    covered with tomato sauce) ··············· 120 NT
Lasagna (Large, flat wheat-flour noodles mixed with
    tomato sauce) ························· 180 NT
Chef's roll (meat rolled into soft shells and covered with
    tomato sauce) ······················ 150 NT
—All orders include garlic bread.

STEP 2 Ask your partner what you could order at his favorite restaurant if

① You dislike spicy foods

_____

② You have false teeth

_____

LESSON 5

(C) LET'S PLAY

● For Student B

Learn the following sentence patterns first, and ask your partner for the information you need.

Does	it this dish	contain have	any very much a lot of	salt meat ? fat

Do	you they	have any	low-calorie vegetarian	dishes ?

What	is chili made of ? is in the lasagna ?

Do you	like prefer	spicy food ? meat ?
Can you eat		dairy products ?

STEP 1   You'd like to invite your partner out for dinner. Tell him about your favorite restaurant.

TaCo Joy   Tex-Mex Grill

Barbecue Sandwiches   beef/porkrib/sausage link ···················· 70 NT

Chili   (a spicy soup made from ground beef, chili
             peppers and sometimes baked beans.) ······················ 30 NT

Tacos   beef/chicken (crisp half-shells made of corn flour,
             holding ground meat with a Mexican hot sauce, lettuce
             and cheese) ·· 30 NT each

Fajitas   beef/chicken (small pieces of meat mixed with stir-fried
             vegetables and wrapped in a soft shell.) ·················· 70 NT

Enceladas   beef/chicken/cheese (meat or cheese wrapped in soft
             shells, soaked in a spicy sauce, and covered with
             cheese.) ··· 60 NT

—All orders include Mexican rice and refried beans.

STEP 2   Ask your partner what you could order at his favorite restaurant if

① You are a vegetarian

_____

② Your partner only has 300 NT dollars

_____

LESSON 5

Exercise

Complete the following dialogue and make your own conversation.

(1) **Dialogue**

- A : Would you like to go out for dinner this evening?
  B : Sure. _____ to.

- A : _____ you come to our party this evening?
  B : It's very _____ you to invite me, but I'm very sorry
  that I _____ on this evening.
  Please ask me again _____ .

- A : _____ you come to a party at my place next Sunday
  night?
  B : That's great. I'd be _____ to.

- A : We are having a little party at my house next week. _____
  _____ you would be able to come with your wife.
  B : Oh, we'd _____ like to. Thank you for _____ us.

(2) **Cartoon**

Lesson 6 How Nice of You to Come

**Listen and repeat
after your teacher.**

(A) LET'S TALK

A : Good afternoon! How nice of you to come.

B : I hope I didn't catch you at a bad time.

A : Oh, no, not at all. Please come in.

B : I haven't seen you in ages.

A : I was going to call on you, but I kept putting it off.

B : Hey! The house looks really nice!

A : Thanks! Please sit down and make yourself at home.

B : Thank you.

A : Would you like a cup of coffee?

B : Don't trouble yourself, please.

LESSON 6

(B) LET'S PRACTICE

Learn the following phrases and do the practice with your partner.

(1) Greeting Guests

1. How nice of you to come.
2. It's nice to have you visit us.
3. I'm so glad you have come.
4. Please come right in.
5. Please leave your shoes here.
6. May I take your coat?
7. They are expecting you.
8. Please make yourself at home.

(2) Coffee or Tea?

9. Would you like something to drink?
10. We have Coca-Cola, orange juice and beer. What would you like?
11. Would you like some refreshments?
12. Which would you prefer, tea or coffee?
13. May I trouble you for another cup of coffee?
14. How would you like your coffee?
15. With sugar, no cream, please.
16. How many spoonfuls of sugar do you like?
17. I take my coffee black.
18. Will you have another cup of coffee?

(3) Help Yourself

19. Help yourself, please.
20. Please help yourself to anything you like.
21. Would you like some more meat?
22. May I have some more?
23. Please have some more.
24. Would you pass me the salt, please?
25. I've enjoyed the dinner very much.
26. How would you like it?
27. This is very delicious.
28. I've had enough, thank you.
29. No more, thank you.

PRACTICE 1

Work in groups of 4. Choose two to be the host and hostess. The others are guests. Practice the following situations. After doing PRACTICE 2, prepare a whole skit to perform for the class.

1. David and Jane pay Mr. and Mrs. Smith a surprise visit.

This old couple offer them something to drink and have a chat with them.

2. Mr. and Mrs. Allen invite Linda and Philip over for dinner. Now the doorbell is ringing.

Mr. and Mrs. Allen prepare some delicious dishes for them.

(4) Leave-Taking

30. It was a pleasure having you.

31. We enjoyed your company.

32. Please come around again.

33. Please take care on your way home.

34. I'm glad you enjoyed it.

35. I'm glad you could come.

36. Can't you stay a little longer?

37. Please come and see us again.

PRACTICE 2

Work in groups of 4. The same as PRACTICE 1.

1. It's about time for David and Jane to leave. Now they are at the door.

2. Philip and Linda had a wonderful meal at the Allens'. Now they are going to leave.

LESSON 6

🎧 (C) LET'S PLAY

● For Student A

Learn the following sentence patterns first, and ask your partner for the information you need.

What else do we	need? have to do?	We	need to should	buy some snacks. borrow a stereo system. send invitations.

If	you I	buy the food,	I'll buy some snacks. could you cook?
When	you're shopping, could you borrow a stereo system? I'm downtown, I'll send invitations.		

- You and your partner are planning a party on Saturday night at 6:30. Think four more things to do with your partner and **divide** the tasks evenly.

THING TO DO:
* buy the food
* send invitations
* borrow a stereo system

- Check your schedule first and decide when you will do them.

FRIDAY			SATURDAY
A.M. Get the car fixed downtown (9:00) P.M. English class (7:00-9:00)			A.M. P.M 6:30 Party!

LESSON 6

🎧 (C) LET'S PLAY

● For Student B

Learn the following sentence patterns first, and ask your partner for the information you need.

What else do we	need? have to do?		We	need to should	buy some snacks. borrow a stereo system. send invitations.

If	you I	buy the food,	I'll buy some snacks.
			could you cook?

When	you're shopping, could you borrow a stereo system? I'm downtown, I'll send invitations.

● You and your partner are planning a party on Saturday night at 6:30. Think four more things to do with your partner and divide the tasks evenly.

THING TO DO:
* buy the food
* send invitations
* borrow a stereo system

● Check your schedule first and decide when you will do them.

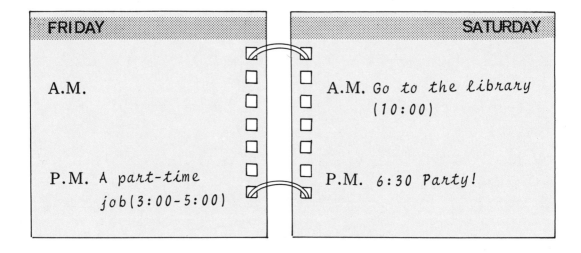

FRIDAY			SATURDAY
A.M.	□	□	A.M. Go to the library (10:00)
	□	□	
	□	□	
	□	□	
P.M. A part-time job (3:00-5:00)	□	□	P.M. 6:30 Party!

LESSON 7

Exercise

Complete the following dialogue, and make up your own conversation.

(1) **Dialogue**

A : Hi, Angela.   I haven't seen you _____ .
B : How nice _____ !   Please _____ .

A : Thank you.
B : Would you like _____ ?

A : Thanks.   Could I _____ , please?
B : Of course.   How _____your coffee?

A : _____ , please.

(2) **Cartoon**

Lesson 7 Please Turn Right at the Next Corner

**Listen and repeat
after your teacher.**

🎧 (A) LET'S TALK

A : Can you take me?
B : Sure. Where to, sir?

A : The Hotel Milton, please.
B : Please hop in.

A : Please turn right at the next corner. Let me out
at the corner.
B : Here you are.

A : How much is the fare?
B : Thirteen dollars and twenty cents.

A : Here you are. Keep the change.
B : Thanks.

LESSON 7

● (B) LET'S PRACTICE

Learn the following phrases and do the practice with your partner.

(1) **The Bus**

1. Where can I get a bus to Central Park?
2. Does this bus go to Market Street?
3. Is this the right bus for Market Street?
4. Where is this bus going?
5. Does this bus stop at the Bank of Taiwan?
6. How many stops to Taipei New Park?
7. Where should I transfer to get to Boston?
8. Where should I get off to go to Hyde Park?
9. Is this seat taken?
10. Please let me off at Kingsbridge.
11. Is this my stop?
12. I missed my stop.

(2) **The Subway**

13. Where do I get a ticket, please?
14. A one-way to Irvington, please.
15. Is this the right train for Irvington?
16. Which train must I take to go to East Side?
17. Which track does the express for Brooklyn leave from?
18. Where is the train going?
19. I took the wrong train.

PRACTICE 1

Work in pairs. A asks the questions below, and B answers according to the route map. Then switch roles.

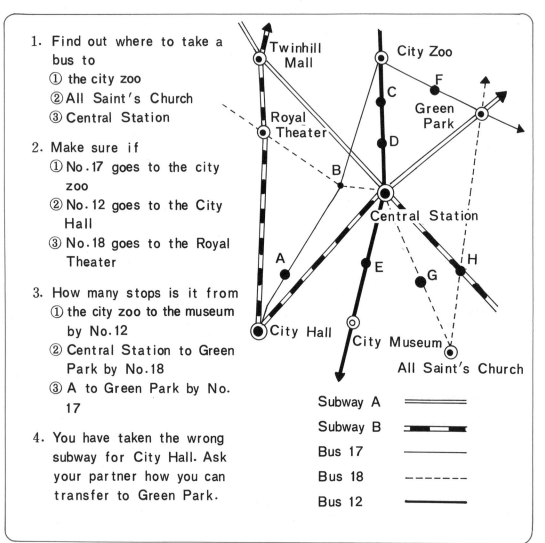

1. Find out where to take a bus to
   ① the city zoo
   ② All Saint's Church
   ③ Central Station

2. Make sure if
   ① No.17 goes to the city zoo
   ② No.12 goes to the City Hall
   ③ No.18 goes to the Royal Theater

3. How many stops is it from
   ① the city zoo to the museum by No.12
   ② Central Station to Green Park by No.18
   ③ A to Green Park by No. 17

4. You have taken the wrong subway for City Hall. Ask your partner how you can transfer to Green Park.

(3) Taxis

20. Where is a taxi stand?

21. Do you know where I can get a taxi?

22. Can you tell me where the taxi stand is?

23. Can you take us to the Hilton Hotel on George Street?

24. Take me to this address, please.

25. Can you put these two bags in the trunk, please?

26. How much will it cost to go to the airport?

27. How much will it be?

28. How long will it take to get there?

29. Make a right turn at the next intersection.

30. Could you stop in front of that white building?

31. Stop here, please.

32. Let me off there, please.

33. Please keep the change.

PRACTICE 2

Work in pairs. One of you is a cabbie, and the other wants a ride. Settle the following before starting the trip: (1) **Fare** (2) **Distance** (3) **Length of time. Then switch roles.**

1. Hilton Hotel on London Street.

2. the airport (with two bags)

3. find the taxi stand first and take a ride to the city museum

LESSON 7

🎧 (C) **LET'S PLAY**   ● For the Whole Class

Learn the following sentence patterns first, and ask your partner for the information you need.

Something is happening		at 3rd Avenue and Maple St.
There's been	an accident a fire a traffic jam	near city Stadium.
I can see	a 20-car pile-up four sawhorses	on 19th St. in the intersection.

The police department The weather bureau City Hall	has	advised warned ordered	drivers	not to drive. to drive slowly.

Take Turn north on	Saxon Lane Loop 900	in order to	avoid bypass	the accident. the traffic jam.

The	road intersection	is	clear. blocked.

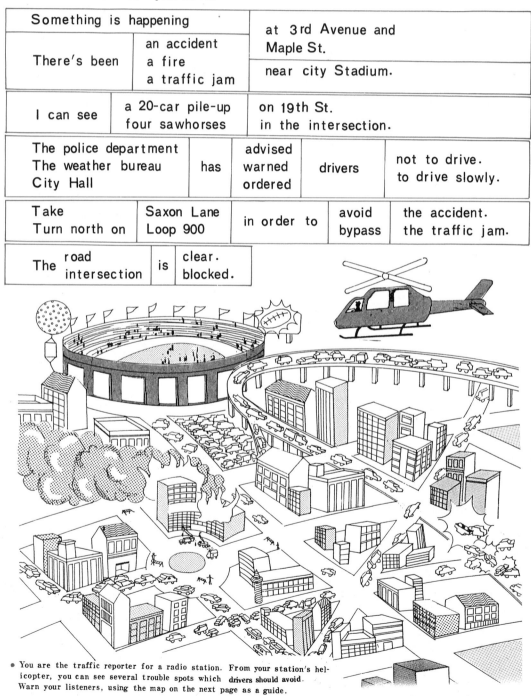

● You are the traffic reporter for a radio station. From your station's helicopter, you can see several trouble spots which drivers should avoid. Warn your listeners, using the map on the next page as a guide.

● **Be sure to mention which roads seem to be clear of obstructions.**

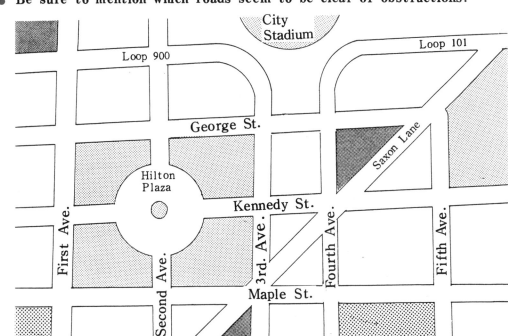

Clues for you

1. Why is there a traffic jam on Loop 101?

2. What's happening near the section of Second Ave. and Kennedy St. ?

3. What's going on at the inter- section of Fourth Ave. and Maple St. ?

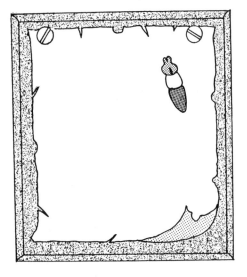

Write down your notes here and report to your listeners.

LESSON 7

Exercise

Complete the following dialogues and make your own conversation.

(1) Dialogue

• A : _____ to go to 5th Avenue?
  B : _____ four or five bucks.

• A : _____ , ma'am?
  B : The city museum.

• A : _____ the Hyde Park, please.
  B : Sure. I'll put _____ here in the back.

• A : _____ to the Fisher Theater?
  B : Take bus No. 1 over there.

• A : _____ for the Fisher Theater?
  B : Yes, please get on.

(2) Cartoon

Lesson 8 How Can I Get to the Station?

**Listen and repeat
after your teacher.**

(A) LET'S TALK

A : Excuse me — how can I get to the train station ?

B : See that intersection up ahead ?

A : Yes, I see it.

B : Turn there. Then watch for a Seven-Eleven.

A : Do I turn at the Seven-Eleven.

B : No, go straight ahead. The station will be on your right.

A : Will I be able to see it from the road ?

B : Sure, you can't miss it.

A : Thanks for your help !

B : Anytime.

🎧 (B) LET'S PRACTICE

Learn the following phrases and do the practice with your partner.

(1) Asking for Directions

1. Excuse me, how can I get to the train station?
2. Excuse me, but could you tell me how to get downtown?
3. Could you tell me the way to Taipei Station?
4. Please tell me the way to Tokyo Station.
5. Which way is the post office, please?
6. Is this the right way to the City Hall?
7. Could you tell me where the Royal Theater is?

(2) Go Straight

8. Go straight along this street.
9. Go straight down this street.
10. Go straight ahead.
11. Keep going until you come to the park.
12. Go to the end of this street.

(3) Take a Turn and Cross

13. Turn right at the second corner.
14. Turn to the right and walk a little.
15. Turn to the left at the second street after you pass the stadium.
16. Cross the bridge and you'll see it on the left.
17. Cross the street there.

PRACTICE 1

Work in pairs. Take turns asking and giving directions. Use the pictures below.

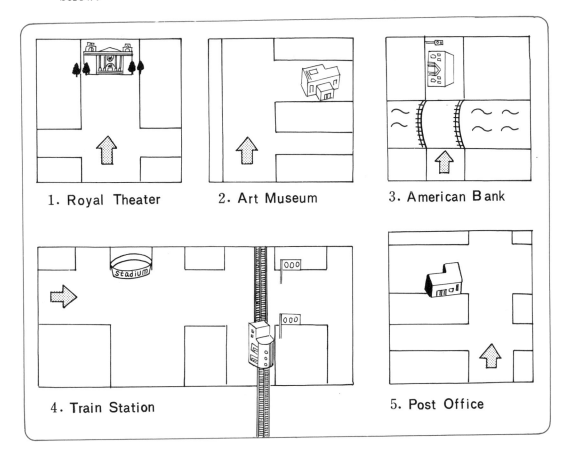

1. Royal Theater

2. Art Museum

3. American Bank

4. Train Station

5. Post Office

(4) **Giving Locations**

18. It's on the left.

19. It's on your right.

20. You'll see it on your right.

21. It's on the corner.

22. It's next to the bank.

23. It's just across the street from a supermarket.

24. It's the second building on your left.

(5) Go Back

25. You've come too far.

26. Go back until you come to the bridge.

27. You'll have to go back a few blocks.

(6) Alternate Responses

28. It's kind of far from here, so you'd better take a bus.

29. I'm sorry, but I'm a stranger around here.

30. Please ask someone else.

31. You'd better ask that policeman over there.

32. I'm going that way myself. I'll take you there.

PRACTICE 2

Work in pairs. Take turns asking and giving directions. Use the pictures below.

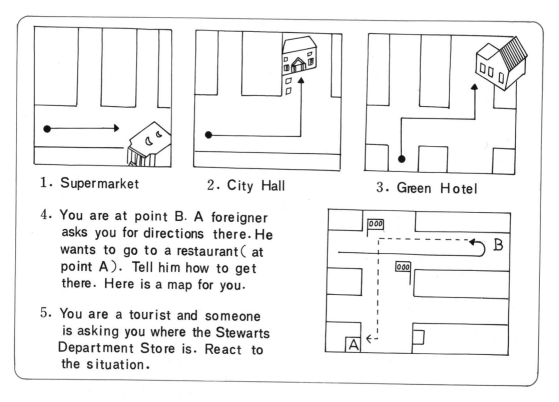

1. Supermarket

2. City Hall

3. Green Hotel

4. You are at point B. A foreigner asks you for directions there. He wants to go to a restaurant (at point A). Tell him how to get there. Here is a map for you.

5. You are a tourist and someone is asking you where the Stewarts Department Store is. React to the situation.

LESSON 8

🧠 (C) LET'S PLAY

● For Student A

Learn the following sentence patterns first, and ask your partner for the information you need.

Excuse me,	could you tell me	where the Royal Theater is?	
		the way to	the Hilton Hotel?
	how can I get to		All Saint's Church?

Go straight	along down	the street	for 2 blocks. , and you'll reach the building. until you come to the 2nd intersection.

Turn	right left	at the second corner. and you'll find it on your left. and walk a little.

It's	on the right. next to the bank. opposite the hotel.	It's	across the street. the second building. on the corner.

● **You have just gotten off the train and arrived at a new town. Ask your partner the way to the following places: ① National Bank ② MacDonald's ③ Royal Theater ④ Parking Lot ⑤ Post Office**
(Write the names on the correct buildings.)

LESSON 8

🎧 (C) LET'S PLAY

● For Student B

Learn the following sentence patterns first, and ask your partner for the information you need.

		where the Royal Theater is?	
Excuse me,	could you tell me	the way to	the Hilton Hotel? All Saint's Church?
	how can I get to		

Go straight	along down	the street	for 2 blocks. , and you'll reach the building. until you come to the 2nd intersection.

Turn	right left	at the second corner. and you'll find it on your left. and walk a little.

It's	on the right. next to the bank. opposite the hotel.	It's	across the street. the second building. on the corner.

● You have just gotten off the train and arrived at a new town. Ask your partner the way to the following places: ① Drugstore ② Department Store ③ High School ④ Hilton Hotel ⑤ Restaurant
(Write the names on the correct buildings.)

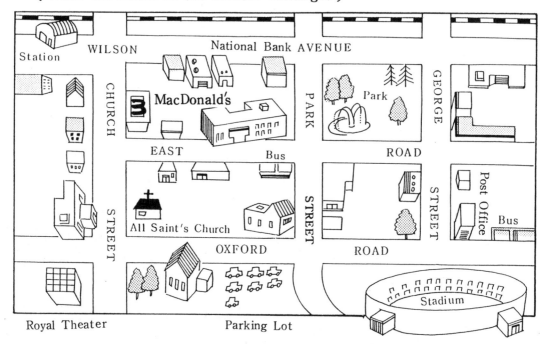

LESSON 8

Exercise

Complete the following dialogue and make your own conversation.

(1) Dialogue

A : Excuse me, but could you tell me _____ get to the
Metropolitan Museum of Art ?

B : Yes, of course. Go straight down _____ and turn
_____ right _____ the second traffic light. It's on the left.
You can't _____ .

A : Thank you very much.

                 *   *   *   *

A : Is this _____ to the City Hall ?

B : Yes, it is.

A : Is it within walking distance ?

B : No, it's kind of _____ here, so _____ .

(2) Cartoon

Lesson 9 What Time Is It?

Listen and repeat
after your teacher.

(A) LET'S TALK

A : Excuse me, what time is it now?
B : It's fifteen after.

A : Um, after two?
B : No, it's 3:15.

A : My watch must be slow.   I'm an hour behind.
B : Well, I set mine to the radio this morning.

A : What time zone are we in?
B : Pacific Time.

A : Hmm, that's what I thought.   I don't understand.
B : Perhaps you have to buy a new watch!

LESSON 9

(B) LET'S PRACTICE

Learn the following phrases and do the practice with your partner.

(1) **Asking the Time**

1. What time is it?
2. What's the time?
3. Do you have the time?
4. What time do you have?
5. What time does your watch say?
6. May I ask you the time?
7. Do you have the correct time?

(2) **Telling the Time**

8. It's about three o'clock.
9. It's 3:00 p.m.
10. It's three ten.
11. It's ten minutes past three.
12. It's three fifteen.
13. It's a quarter past three.
14. It's three thirty.
15. It's half past three.
16. It's three forty-five.
17. It's a quarter to four.
18. It's exactly twenty minutes and ten seconds past three o'clock.

PRACTICE 1

Work in pairs.   Using the chart above, ask your partner what time it is in ① New York ② Hawaii ③ Cairo ④ Budapest ⑤ Madrid ⑥ Buenos Aires ⑦ London.

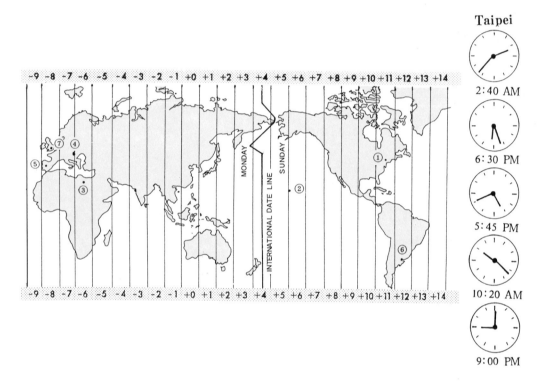

Taipei

2:40 AM

6:30 PM

5:45 PM

10:20 AM

9:00 PM

(3) The Date

19. What's today?

20. What day is today?

21. What year is this?

22. What day of the month is it today?

23. What day of the week is it today?

24. Today is April the fifth.

25. It is the 28th of May.

26. It is 1989.

27. It's Tuesday.

(4) **Frequency and Duration**

28. How many times a year do you go there?

29. How often do you go there?

30. I usually go there.

31. I go there every other day.

32. I go there every three days.

33. I go there nearly every week.

34. I go there once a year.

35. I seldom go there.

36. I never go there.

PRACTICE 2

Work in pairs. Think 3 more well-known dates and ask your partner.

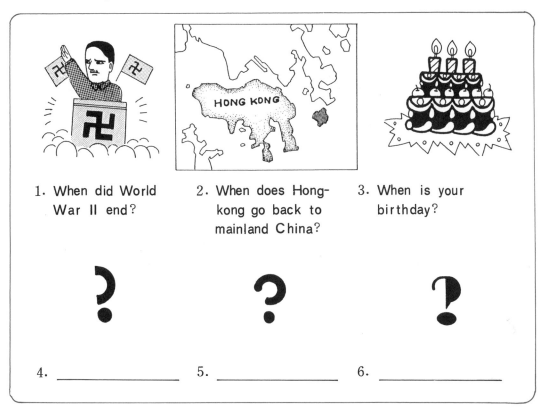

1. When did World War II end?

2. When does Hong-kong go back to mainland China?

3. When is your birthday?

4. _____   5. _____   6. _____

LESSON　9

🎤 (C) LET'S PLAY

● For Student　A

Learn the following sentence patterns first, and ask your partner for the information you need.

How often do you	eat at MacDonald's?
Do you ever	clean your shoes?

I	always often sometimes hardly ever never	eat at MacDonalds. clean my shoes.

I	eat at MacDonald's clean my shoes	once a week. twice a month. every Tuesday night.

● Work in pairs. Use the sentence patterns above to complete the tables.

How often do you·········

Get a haircut	You:
	Your partner:
	Tony: every 2 weeks
	Mary:

Read the paper	You:
	Your partner:
	Tony: everyday
	Mary:

Go to the movies	You:
	Your partner:
	Tony:
	Mary: twice a month

Go shopping	You:
	Your partner:
	Tony: hardly ever
	Mary:

Play pachinko	You:
	Your partner:
	Tony:
	Mary: never

Watch TV	You:
	Your partner:
	Tony:
	Mary: sometimes

Go to the dentist	You:
	Your partner:
	Tony:
	Mary: hardly ever

Cook for yourself	You:
	Your partner:
	Tony:
	Mary: every Tuesday night

LESSON 9

🎧 (C) LET'S PLAY　　　　　● For Student B

Learn the following sentence patterns first, and ask your partner for the information you need.

How often do you Do you ever	eat at MacDonald's? clean your shoes?

I	always often sometimes hardly ever never	eat at MacDonalds. clean my shoes.

I	eat at MacDonald's clean my shoes	once a week. twice a month. every Tuesday night.

● **Work in pairs. Use the sentence patterns above to complete the tables.**

How often do you········

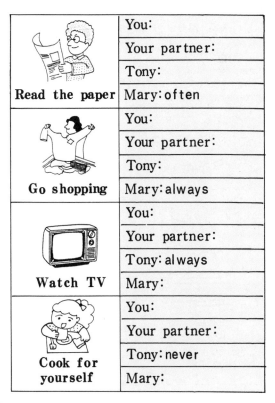

Get a haircut	You:
	Your partner:
	Tony:
	Mary: never

Go to the movies	You:
	Your partner:
	Tony: often
	Mary:

Play pachinko	You:
	Your partner:
	Tony: every Sunday
	Mary:

Go to the dentist	You:
	Your partner:
	Tony: once a year
	Mary:

Read the paper	You:
	Your partner:
	Tony:
	Mary: often

Go shopping	You:
	Your partner:
	Tony:
	Mary: always

Watch TV	You:
	Your partner:
	Tony: always
	Mary:

Cook for yourself	You:
	Your partner:
	Tony: never
	Mary:

LESSON 9

Exercise

Fill in the blanks.

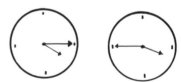

1. A : Do you have the time?

   B : It's a _____ four.
   It's a _____ four.
   It's _____ .
   It's _____ three.

2. A : How often do you wash your hair?

   B : I wash it _____ .
   I wash it _____ .
   I wash it _____ .
   I wash it _____ .

M	T	W	Th	F	S	S
√	√	√	√	√	√	
√		√		√		√
√			√			√
√						

3. A : How often do you eat at home?

   B : _____ .
   _____ .
   _____ .
   _____ .

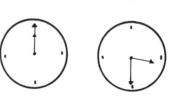

(100%)   (50%)

(90%)   (0%)

4. **Cartoon**

Lesson 10 It's a Beautiful Day

**Listen and repeat
after your teacher.**

(A) LET'S TALK

A : It's a beautiful day, isn't it?
B : It sure is. Spring came early this year.

A : It looks like it's going to be a hot summer.
B : I hope not.

A : Does it get this hot in your country?
B : Yes, but there's not so much humidity.

A : They say it's supposed to rain this afternoon.
B : Is it really? I missed the weather forecast.

A : The weatherman is usually wrong anyway.
B : In this climate you just can't tell.

LESSON 10

🎧 (B) LET'S PRACTICE

Learn the following phrases and do the practice with your partner.

(1) **Talking about the Weather**

1. How is the weather today?
2. It's very good.
3. It's raining.
4. It's very windy.
5. It's getting cloudy.
6. It's very hot.
7. It's cold enough to snow.
8. How was the weather in Paris yesterday?
9. It was 19° centigrade, and it was cloudy and windy.

PRACTICE 1

Work in pairs. Ask and answer questions about the chart.

Today's Weather		Yesterday's Weather	
1. London 18°C	cloudy	1. Taipei 18°C	windy
2. Paris 20°C	sunny & warm	2. Hualien 21°C	stormy & rainy
3. Cairo 32°C	sunny & hot	3. Kaohsiung 33°C	muggy
4. Dallas 22°C	rainy	4. Tainan 20°C	breezy
5. Tokyo 12°C	cloudy & cool	5. Taichung 16°C	foggy & cool

(2) **Spring**

10. What a beautiful day it is today!

11. Isn't it a lovely day?

12. It's a beautiful day, isn't it?

13. Beautiful weather, isn't it?

14. Yes. It couldn't be better.

15. Yes, indeed! It's really spring.

16. The days are getting warmer.

17. The sun is certainly warm enough now.

18. It's nice to have some spring weather.

19. I hope this weather will last for a few more days.

20. The fog is very dense, isn't it?

(3) Summer

21. It looks like rain, doesn't it?

22. It's raining again.

23. Has the rainy season set in already?

24. We're going to have a typhoon tomorrow, I hear.

25. We've been having so much rain these days.

26. The rainy season is here.

27. It's very hot and humid, isn't it?

28. It's very warm today, isn't it?

29. What a hot day!

30. There is hardly any wind today.

31. It's very damp, so the heat is unbearable.

32. I'm all in a sweat!

(4) Fall & Winter

33. It's very cold this morning, isn't it?

34. It's very cold for this time of year, isn't it?

35. It's chilly tonight, isn't it?

36. It's going to snow, isn't it?

37. Nasty day, isn't it?

38. What a heavy storm we had last night!

39. It has turned cold, hasn't it?

40. It's biting cold. The wind is like a knife.

41. We had severe frost.

PRACTICE 2

Work in pairs. Start a conversation by talking about the weather today. Use the situations below.

1. sunny   2. cloudy   3. rainy

4. windy and cold   5. breezy   6. snowy

7. foggy and chilly   8. hot and humid   9. stormy

LESSON 10

🎧 (C) LET'S PLAY

● For Student A

Learn the following sentence patterns first, and ask your partner for the information you need.

What's the temperature	in Baker for tomorrow?	The current temperature will be 79° Fahrenheit.
How about the temperature		Tomorrow's temperature will reach 72°F.

What's the weather forecast for	Burns Salem	for tomorrow?
What does the weatherman say about	Burns? Salem?	

The weather	report forecast	says	it	will be foggy and cloudy.
			is going to	rain tomorrow.
				clear up in the afternoon.
It		we will have drizzle tomorrow.		

● **Complete the chart below.**

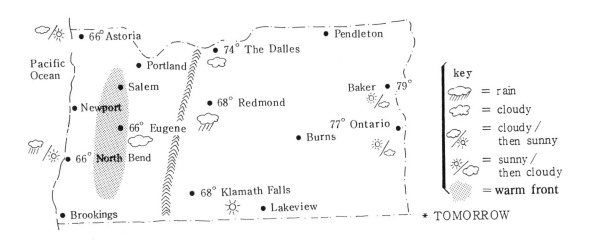

key
🌧 = rain
☁ = cloudy
☁/☀ = cloudy / then sunny
☀/☁ = sunny / then cloudy
▦ = warm front

* TOMORROW

● **According to the information above, draw up a weather forecast for North Bend. Then compare yours with your partner's.**

LESSON 10

🎧 (C) LET'S PLAY

● For Student B

Learn the following sentence patterns first, and ask your partner for the information you need.

What's the temperature	in Baker for tomorrow?	The current temperature will be 79° Fahrenheit.
How about the temperature		Tomorrow's temperature will reach 72°F.

What's the weather forecast for	Burns / Salem	for tomorrow?
What does the weatherman say about	Burns? / Salem?	

The weather	report forecast	says	it	will be foggy and cloudy.
			is going to	rain tomorrow.
				clear up in the afternoon.
It			we will have drizzle tomorrow.	

● **Complete the chart below.**

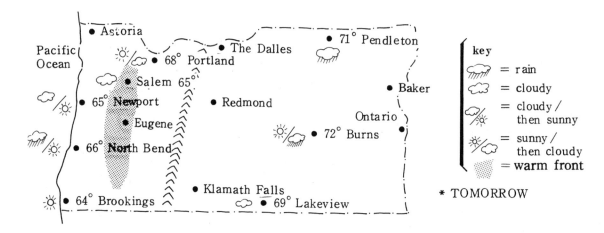

● **According to the information above, draw up a weather forecast for North Bend. Then compare yours with your partner's.**

LESSON 10

Exercise

Complete the following dialogue and make your own conversation.

(1) **Dialogue**

A : It's very_____, isn't it ?
B : Yes, it certainly is.

A : It's a lovely day today,_____?
B : Yes. It couldn't_____.

A : _____ the weatherman_____?
B : He says it'll_____by this evening.

A : _____ ?
B : The current temperature today is $26°$ centigrade.

A : It's very_____today, isn't it ?
B : Terribly hot! It's very_____so the heat is_____.

(2) **Cartoon**

Lesson 11 I'm Going to Europe

**Listen and repeat
after your teacher.**

🎧 (A) LET'S TALK

A : How much vacation time do you get?

B : Only two weeks this year, but three weeks next year.

A : We get four weeks a year after five years of service.

B : So where do you plan to go for your vacation, Steve?

A : I'm going to Europe. What about you?

B : I'm going to visit some old friends in Florida.

A : And when will you be back?

B : Probably in about a week and a half.

A : Well, I hope you have a good vacation.

B : You too, Steve.

LESSON 11

(B) LET'S PRACTICE

Learn the following phrases and do the practice with your partner.

(1) **In the Airplane**

1. Would you show me to my seat?
2. May I change my seat?
3. May I have something to read?
4. Do you have any Chinese weekly magazines?
5. Do you have a Chinese newspaper?
6. Please show me how to fasten my seat belt.
7. What is this button for?
8. How can I turn the light?
9. A blanket and a pillow, please.
10. I don't feel well. Please give me some medicine.
11. May I have an air-sickness bag?
12. Shall I get some water?
13. What channel is the movie on?
14. What kind of movie can we see today?
15. Can I have an earphone, please?

PRACTICE 1

A role-play for the whole class.

❖ All of you are in an airplane. The teacher plays the flight attendant. Every passenger will bother the friendly flight attendant for help. Let's take off!

● **Information**

brandy   red wine   white wine   coffee

tea   milk   a refill   whisky on the rocks   beer

cigarettes   match   orange juice   tomato juice

coke   water   hot (cold) towel   a pack of cards   earphones

(2) **At the Customs**

airsick bag

magazine

newspaper

16. May I see your passport?

17. Here's my passport.

18. How long are you going to stay in the United States?

19. I'll stay here for about two weeks.

20. What is the purpose of your visit?

21. For sightseeing.

22. I'm here on business.

23. I'm in a tourist group.

24. To visit my friends.

25. To see my relative.

26. To attend the summer school.

27. Do you have anything to declare?

28. I have nothing to declare.

29. I only have my personal effects.

30. There are some gifts for my friends.

31. These are for my own use.

PRACTICE 2

A role-play for the whole class.

◆ All of you are off the plane and at the customs counter. The teacher is supposed to be a customs officer. Fill in the card below, then wait in line with your luggage and passport.

ROLE - CARD

- Name: _____
- Date of Birth: _____
- Nationality: _____
- Occupation: _____
- Duration of Stay: _____
- Purpose of Stay: _____
- Items to carry: _____
- Destination: _____

● **You must take one of the items below with you.**

(3) **In the Hotel**

32. I'd like to check in, please.

33. I have a reservation for two nights from today.

34. Do you have a room available for tonight?

35. Can I have a room, please?

36. Is there a room with a nice view?

37. I'd like a single room with a bath, please.

38. What kind of room would you like?

39. What's the rate for a twin room?

40. How much is it for one night?

41. What are the room rates?

PRACTICE 3

A role-play for the whole class.

❖ Now all of you have passed through customs and are on your way to a hotel. Here is the check-in counter of the hotel. Your teacher is supposed to be the clerk. Fill in the form below, then begin to check in.

●**Information**

ROLE CARD
· Name : _____
· Reservations? _____
· How Many People with You

_____
· Condition of Room

_____
· Duration of Stay

_____

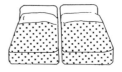

double   single

twin

LESSON 11

🎧 (C) LET'S PLAY

● For Student A

Learn the following sentence patterns first, and ask your partner for the information you need.

What did they do	in Yellowstone National Park?
How did they get there?	

They	went skiing. went to a casino. fed the bears.

They	went there by	bus. plane. car.
	drove a rented car.	

● Find out where the Smith family went on vacation. You know some of the places they went and things they did. Your partner knows the rest. Here are some clues, numbered in the order that they happened.

1	2	3	4
San Francisco, California		Flagstaff, Arizona	
5	6	7	8
Dallas, Texas		Mt. Rushmore, Wyoming	

● **Here are the places where your partner knows what they did:**

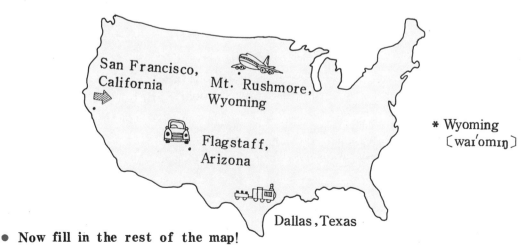

San Francisco, California

Mt. Rushmore, Wyoming

Flagstaff, Arizona

Dallas, Texas

＊ Wyoming 〔waiʹomɪŋ〕

● **Now fill in the rest of the map!**

LESSON 11

🎧 (C) LET'S PLAY

● For Student B

Learn the following sentence patte s first, and ask your partner for the information you need.

What did they do	in Yellowstone National Park?
How did they get there?	

● Find out where the Smith family went on vacation. You know some of the places they went and things they did. Your partner knows the rest. Here are some clues, numbered in the order that they happened.

They	went skiing. went to a casino. fed the bears.	
They	went there by	bus. plane. car.
	drove a rented car.	

1	2	3	4
	Las Vegas, Nevada		Albuquerque, New Mexico
5		7	8
Southfork Ranch	Boulder, Colorado		Yellowstone National Park

● **Here are the places when your partner knows what they did:**

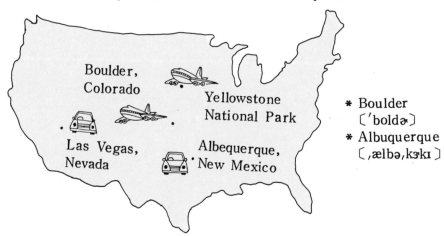

Boulder, Colorado
Yellowstone National Park
Las Vegas, Nevada
Albequerque, New Mexico

* Boulder [ˈboldɚ]
* Albuquerque [ˌælbəˌkɚkɪ]

● **Now fill in the rest of the map!**

LESSON 11

Exercise

Complete the following dialogues and make your own conversation.

① A : Good morning, sir.

B : Hello. Can you _____ ?

A : _____. 24B. Your seat is this way.

It's an _____ on the right.

B : Thank you.

          *   *   *

② A : Your passport, please.

B : Yes. _____.

A : _____ of your trip?

B : I'm here _____.

A : How long _____ ?

B : _____.

          *   *   *

③ A : Good afternoon. Can I help you?

B : Do you _____ ?

A : Yes, sir, we do. _____ a single room or
a double room ?

B : A single room, please.
_____ ?

A : Single rooms are eighty-five
dollars a night.

Lesson 12 Let Me Show You Around

**Listen and repeat
after your teacher.**

🎧 (A) LET'S TALK

A : Hello. You're here about the apartment, aren't you?

B : Yes. We talked over the phone last week, remember?

A : Come on in. Let me show you around.

B : It seems kind of small.

A : There are two bedrooms and a living room. And one bath.

B : How are you fixed for closet space?

A : Oh, each bedroom has a large closet.

B : And the rent?

A : Four hundred dollars a month, plus utilities.

B : That's very reasonable.

LESSON 12

(B) LET'S PRACTICE

Learn the following phrases and do the practice with your partner.

(1) **Asking Around**

1. I'd like to rent an apartment.

2. I'd like to take a look at the apartment you advertised in today's paper.

3. I'm calling about the apartment you're advertising.

4. Sure, what would you like to know?

5. Where is the apartment?

6. I would like to come by to see the apartment.

7. Can I see the room now?

8. I'd like to make an appointment to see the place.

(2) **Looking Around**

9. How big is it?

10. Is it near a school?

11. Is there a shopping center nearby?

12. Is it furnished?

13. How many bedrooms are there in this house?

14. This apartment has two bedrooms and a combination dining room-kitchen.

15. Here are the bedrooms. There is a bathroom between them.

16. The living room faces south and is very warm in winter.

17. The house is located near a bus stop.

18. Does the apartment have a good view?

19. This is a well-furnished room.

20. The oven and refrigerator are included.

21. Does the house have air-conditioning?

22. Is there a heater in this house?

23. What is the basement used for?

PRACTICE 1

Work in pairs. One of you is the landlord, and the other is the renter. Take turns making appointments by phone to see the apartments below. Be sure to get the exact address before you hang up. You can ask anything else you want to know.

CLASSIFIED ADVERTISEMENTS

CHINA NEWS 24 JULY

Want to learn CHINESE?
Chinese painting or calligraphy?
Tutor, Individual & Group   TEL:781-9768

CHINESE STUDYING government recongized school, 1500/8 Wks. no waiting. no visa worries, Address: 2nd Floor, No. 126-8, Hsin-Sheng South Road Section 1 Tel: 394-5400

DAILY TEL: 8363637—9

INTERNATIONAL REALTY
HOUSE OR APARTMENT FOR RENT

4F 37 Teh-hain E Rd Tienmou

Room-mate wanted. Call 706-8065 at 7:00 pm.

Apartments For Rent

For rent — East district Taipei near Tun Hwa N. Rd., 20 pings furnished, NT$18,000 monthly. Tel: 821-5152.

Fully furnished apartment for rent, tasteful decor., nice environment, large garden, good security 836-0815 Jane

3 bed rooms furnished apartment Sin-Yi Rd. 773-1836 Tom.

DRUMMER & BASSIST
to play blues/ rock Contact John at 394-0384

(3) **Talking About the Rent**

24. What's the monthly rent?

25. How much is the rent?

26. Four hundred dollars a month, plus utilities.

27. The rent is 400 U.S. dollars a month.

28. Are utilities included in the rent?

29. How much is the security deposit?

(4) **Thinking It Over**

30. It seems a little too small for us.

31. I need some time to think it over.

32. I'm sorry, but it's just not what we're looking for.

33. We want to rent it.

34. I'll take this room.

35. Thanks a million for showing us around.

PRACTICE 2

Work in pairs.   Read the role-cards below, then take turns playing the roles.

landlords		renters
1. 400 U.S. dollars per month plus utilities		would like to take this room and move in soon
2. 2 bedrooms and 1 bath, no airconditioning		too small, want to think it over
3. the monthly rent is 700 U.S. but is flexible		not within the price range, try to make the rent lower
4. newly painted but no pets allowed.	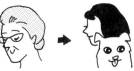	have a dog, not satisfied, not planning to rent this room.

LESSON 12

🎧 (C) LET'S PLAY

● For Student A

Learn the following sentence patterns, and ask your partner for the information you need.

How many	bedrooms bathrooms telephones	are there	in the house? in the apartment?

Is there	a grocery store a shopping center a bus line	nearby?

A bus line A grocery store	is just	a block a few minutes	away.	Are they Is it	furnished? carpeted?

Does	the house the apartment the room	have	a good view? air-conditioning? central-heating?	What about	the neighborhood? the bedrooms? the kitchen?

1. You want to rent an apartment. You saw this advertisement in the newspaper. Call to find out more about the apartment.

> Newly painted apartment near Tienmou for rent, good view, good security, 15000 NT per month plus utilities, 9047872
> Miss Wang

MEMO

rooms: ＿＿＿＿＿＿＿＿

furniture: ＿＿＿＿＿＿＿＿

neighborhood: ＿＿＿＿＿＿

other: ＿＿＿＿＿＿＿＿＿

2. You have an apartment you want to rent. Your partner telephones to ask about the apartment.

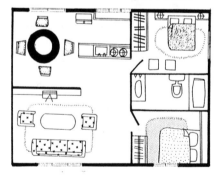

★ More details for you

1. living room: ceiling fan, new sofa
2. quiet neighborhood, off the street
3. near a bus line
4. third floor walk-up, no pet
5. apartment complex: swimming pool and tennis court
6. a combination dining room-kitchen

LESSON 12

(C) LET'S PLAY

• For Student B

Learn the following sentence patterns, and ask your partner for the information you need.

How many	bedrooms bathrooms telephones	are there	in the house? in the apartment?			

Is there	a grocery store a shopping center a bus line	nearby?				

A bus line A grocery store	is just	a block a few minutes	away.	Are they Is it	furnished? carpeted?

Does	the house the apartment the room	have	a good view? air-conditioning? central-heating?	What about	the neighborhood? the bedrooms? the kitchen?

2. You want to rent an apartment. You saw this advertisement in the newspaper. Call to find out more about the apartment.

> 2 bedrooms furnished apartment Sin-yi Road, no pets, nice environment and convenient transportation, 20000 call 7315172 David

MEMO

rooms: _____

furniture: _____

neighborhood: _____

other: _____

1. You have an apartment you want to rent. Your partner telephones to ask about the apartment.

★ More detail for you

1. space for air-conditioning
2. living room: a set of comfortable chairs, wall to wall carpeting
3. stove and refrigerator in kitchen
4. on the 10th floor
5. near a shopping center
6. 24-hour security guard

LESSON 12

Exercise

Complete the following dialogue and make your own conversation.

(1) **Dialogue**

- A : Hello, I'm here about _____ .
  B : Come in. Let me _____ .

- A : How much _____ ?
  B : $ 300 a month, plus _____ .

- A : Does this apartment have _____ ?
  B : No, but there are ceiling fans.

- A : How many rooms are there in this house?
  B : This apartment has _____ and _____

  _____ .

(2) **Cartoon**

Lesson 13   I Totally Agree With You

**Listen and repeat
after your teacher.**

(A) LET'S TALK

A : We're impressed by your company, but there's one problem.

B : What's that?

A : Some of us feel your company may be too small.

B : I totally agree with you. That's why we're expanding.

A : What about in the meantime?

B : Well, since we don't have so many customers, we'll work extra hard on your company's project.

A : Hmm. Let me get back to you on this, okay? I'm afraid the management will be hard to convince.

B : Of course. Take all the time you need.

LESSON 13

🎧 (B) LET'S PRACTICE

Learn the following phrases and do the practice with your partner.

(1) Disagreement

1. On the contrary.
2. By no means.
3. I don't think so.
4. I don't agree with you.
5. I disagree.
6. I rather doubt it.
7. You don't say so !
8. I object to it.
9. Of course not.
10. Certainly not.
11. Definitely not.
12. Absolutely no way.
13. I'm afraid I don't agree with you.

14. I can't agree to your proposal.
15. Well, I doubt it !
16. I'm afraid you're mistaken.
17. I'm afraid not.
18. I think otherwise.
19. I can't go along with what you said.
20. I'm sorry but I have to disagree with you.
21. I don't believe so.
22. What you said does not make sense.
23. That's very unlikely.

PRACTICE 1

Work in pairs. Take turns giving and disagreeing with the opinions below. Try to use as many different phrases as possible.

1. We had better put it off until a week from now.
2. A woman's place is in the home.
3. Sports are a waste of time.
4. English is very difficult / easy.
5. Television is the greatest / worst invention of the twentieth century.

(2) **Agreement**

24. Oh, yes.
25. Why not ?
26. Right.
27. Exactly.
28. Absolutely.
29. Sure.
30. It's true.
31. That's right.
32. Quite so.
33. Indeed it is.
34. You're quite right.
35. I agree with you.
36. I think so, too.

37. That's it.
38. Of course.
39. I agree.
40. You're right.
41. You can say that again.
42. You got it.
43. You bet.
44. That's just what I was going to say.
45. I totally agree with you.
46. That's just what I wanted to say.

PRACTICE 2

Work in pairs. Take turns giving and agreeing with the opinions below. Try to use as many different phrases as possible.

1. Dennis is very easy to talk with.
2. Tom's sister is very charming.
3. Taipei is one of the most fascinating cities in the world.
4. The lifetime employment system is good.
5. Sports are good for health.

LESSON 13

🎧 **(C) LET'S PLAY**   ●For the Whole Class

Learn the following sentence patterns first, and do the activity with your classmates.

I	don't	believe think	so,	because......
	disagee, am against that, can't go along with what you said,			

I'm afraid	I can't agree with you. you're mistaken. that's very unlikely. I have to disagree with you.

What you said	does not make sense. is totally wrong.

Debating

●**For the Teacher**

As a class, pick a controversial issue to argue about. Then divide into two teams representing two sides of the issue (for and against). The two sides should take turns responding to each other's opinions. No person should speak twice unless everyone else has spoken at least once.

● Here are some ideas for debating topics. Feel free to choose your own, however.

The Environment

The Role of Women

To Marry or Not to Marry

LESSON 13

🎧 (C) LET'S PLAY

●Work in Pairs

Learn the following sentence patterns first, and do the activity with your partner.

Alice Maggie	is	her his	mother. granddaughter.	Gail Chris He	is	her his	brother's uncle's	cousin. niece. son. cousin.
Bob			uncle.					

They are He's my	half-	brothers, brother,	because	their mother divorced. our father remarried.

● Work in pairs. Take turns selecting any two of the people below.
Then ask your partner what their relationship is. For example:

A: How are Maggie and Tony related?

B: They're sister and brother.

(Julie's 2nd marriage)

(Julie's 1st marriage)

Arthur   Julie   Arnold   Steve   Alice

Gail   Don   Betty   Bob   Ben   Maria   Bert

Chris   Maggie   Tony   Paula   Jill

● Useful Terms

husband	grandfather	ex-wife	stepdaughter	father-in-law
ex-husband	son	mother	brother	brother-in-law
child	grandson	stepmother	half-brother	son-in-law
father	stepson	grandmother	uncle	aunt/siblings
stepfather	wife	granddaughter	nephew	niece/cousins

LESSON 13

Exercise

Complete the following dialogues and make your own conversation.

(1) **Dialogue**

- A : I reckon him to be the best pianist in the world.
  B : _____ .

- A : The task is too tough for Mary.
  B : I'm afraid _____ .

- A : Maybe he'll come to apologize.
  B : _____ .

- A : Elizabeth Taylor is the most attractive woman in the world.
  B : _____ .

- A : Woman are as intelligent as men.
  B : _____ .

(2) **Cartoon**

Lesson 14 Review

(A) LET'S WRITE

Fill in the blanks and make your own conversation.

1

A : I lost _____ .

B : What's your name please ?

A : Bob Young.

B : Could you _____ ?

A : Sure — it's brown leather, about so big.

B : _____ did you have inside ?

A : About fifty dollars. Plus my _____ and all my credit cards.

2

A : _____ go out together sometime ?

B : I'd _____ to. _____ to go out ?

A : Are you free this weekend ?

B : Well, I have classes on Friday, but I'm free after that.

A : Great! Then _____ dinner and a movie ?

B : Sounds _____ .

3

B : Hello, _____ Lisa Welch. _____ to Mr. Davis ?

A : I'm sorry, but Mr. Davis _____ .

B : Do you know _____?

A : Maybe later today. May I _____?

B : Okay. Just tell him that Lisa Welch called.

A : Got it.

4

A : Operator. _____?

B : I'd like to _____ to the United States, please.

A : What number, please?

B : Area code (817) 485-0306.

A : And your name?

B : John.

A : _____, please. (The phone rings.)

C : Hello?

A : You have a collect call from John. Will you _____ _____?

C : Yes, I will.

A : Your party is _____ . Please _____.

5

A : Do you have any plans for tomorrow evening? Say around six?

B : Not yet. Why _____?

A : My parents _____ dinner.

B : Thanks ... _____ !

A : They're _____ meeting you.

B : It was really _____ .

6

A : Good afternoon! _____ of you to come.

B : I hope I didn't _____ .

A : Oh, no, not _____ . Please come in.

B : I haven't seen you for ages.

A : I was going to call on you, but I _____ .

B : Hey! The house looks really nice!

A : Thanks! Please sit down and _____ yourself _____ .

7

A : Can you take us?

B : Sure _____ , sir?

A : The Hotel Milton, please.

B : Please hop in.

    *   *   *   *

A : Please _____ at the next corner. Let us _____ at the corner.

B : Here you are.

8

A : _____ , _____ get to the train station?

B : See that intersection up _____ ?

A : Yes, I see it.

B : Turn there. Then _____ a 7-11.

A : Do I turn at the 7-11?

B : No, go _____ . The station will be ____ your right.

9

A : Excuse me, _____ now ?

B : It's fifteen after three.

A : My watch must be slow. I'm an hour _____ .

B : Well, I _____ mine _____ this morning.

10

A : _____ ?

B : It sure is. Spring came early this year.

A : It _____ it's going to be a hot summer.

B : I hope not.

A : Does_____ get this hot in your country ?

B : Yes, but _____ .

11

A : _____ vacation time do you get ?

B : Only two weeks this year, but three weeks next year.

A : So where do you plan to_____ your vacation ?

B : I'm going to _____ .

A : Well, I hope _____ .

12

A : Hello. You're here about the apartment, _____ ?

B : Yes. We talked _____ last week.

A : Come on in. Let me _____ .

B : It seems _____ of small.

A : There are two bedrooms and a living room. And one bath.

B : And the rent ?

A : Four hundred dollars a month, _____ .

13

A : We're impressed ____your company, but there's one problem.

B : _____ ?

A : Some of us feel your company may be too small.

B : I _____ you. That's why we're expanding.

LESSON 14

🎧 (B) LET'S PLAY

Read the following directions and do the role play.

1. Work in a group of three. Decide who will be A, B and C.

2. Each of you reads the activity card for your own part only. No peeking!

3. When you finish Activity 1, go on to Activity 2, and so on.

4. If you like, you can perform the skit again for the whole class.

ROLE CARD [1]

A

You are flying to New York on business. Now you are going to pass through customs.

B

Here are your roles:
① policeman in the airport
② manager of Roger's Company in N.Y.
③ A's boss David Wang in Taipei
④ A's old friend in N.Y., Mike Lee

C

Here are your roles:
① customs officer
② taxi driver
③ clerk in the Hotel
④ operator
⑤ Jason Hong, boss of Roger's Company
⑥ Mike Lee's wife Vicky

ROLE ACTIVITY CARDS

A₁

After passing the customs, you find your wallet has been stolen. Try to find a policeman.

A₂

Get your wallet back and call the manager of Roger's company to pick you up.

A₃

You and B are in a taxi. You ask B about the weather here.

B₁

You are a policeman in the airport. You know there is a wallet at the Lost & Found. See whether it is A's wallet.

B₂

You are the manager. Wait for the phone to ring. Then welcome A and get a taxi to the hotel with A.

B₃

React to the situation.

C₁

You are the customs officer. Do your duty.

C₂

You are the taxi driver. Take A and B to the Green Hotel.

C₃

You tell them the weather forecast for tomorrow.

A₄
You and B arrive at the Hotel. You've already made reservations. Now check in.

B₄
Make an appointment with A for a meeting at 10:00 tomorrow morning.

C₄
You are the clerk in the Hotel. React to the situation.

A₅
Make a collect call to your boss in Taipei from your room.

B₅
You are David Wang. Wait for the phone to ring.

C₅
You are the front desk clerk and operator again in this activity. Help A.

You have a good night's sleep, and now it's time for the meeting.

A₆
You represent your company, and offer a cooperation plan in the meeting.

B₆
You are the manager again. Agree and disagree with certain parts of the plan.

C₆
You are the boss of Roger's Company. Make a final decision on this plan.

A₇
Reject C's invitation with an excuse and set an alternative time. Then ask B how to get to Maple Steet where your old friend Mike lives.

B₇
Draw A a map and give directions.

C₇
After the meeting, you invite A over for dinner tonight.

A₈
Pay a surprise visit to your old friend Mike and his wife Vicky.

B₈
You are Mike Lee. You haven't seen A for 3 years. React to the situation.

C₈
You are Mike's wife. Offer A something to drink.

Have a nice chat !

 心得筆記欄

特別推薦

全國最完整的文法書 ☆ ☆ ☆

文法寶典

▶ 劉 毅 編著

　　這是一套想學好英文的人必備的工具書，作者積多年豐富的教學經驗，針對大家所不了解和最容易犯錯的地方，編寫成一套完整的文法書。

　　本書編排方式與眾不同，首先給讀者整體的概念，再詳述文法中的細節部分，內容十分完整。文法說明以圖表為中心，一目了然，並且務求深入淺出。無論您在考試中或其他書中所遇到的任何不了解的問題，或是您感到最煩惱的文法問題，查閱**文法寶典**均可迎刃而解。例如：哪些副詞可修飾名詞或代名詞？(P.228)；什麼是介副詞？(P.543)；那些名詞可以當副詞用？(P.100)；倒裝句 (P.629)、省略句 (P.644) 等特殊構句，為什麼倒裝？為什麼省略？原來的句子是什麼樣子？在**文法寶典**裏都有詳盡的說明。

　　例如，有人學了**觀念錯誤的**「假設法現在式」的公式，

> If + 現在式動詞……，主詞 + shall (will, may, can) + 原形動詞

只會造：If it rains, I will stay at home.

而不敢造：If you *are* right, I *am* wrong.

　　　　　If I *said* that, I *was* mistaken.

　　　　　（If 子句不一定用在假設法，也可表示條件子句的直說法。）

可見如果學文法不求徹底了解，反而成為學習英文的絆腳石，對於這些易出錯的地方，我們都特別加以說明 (詳見 P.356)。

　　文法寶典每冊均附有練習，只要讀完本書、做完練習，您必定信心十足，大幅提高對英文的興趣與實力。

◉ **全套五冊**，**售價900元**。市面不售，請直接向本公司購買。

●5分鐘學會說英文①②③冊●

張　齡　編譯

「**五分鐘學會説英文**」是根據美國中央情報局的特殊記憶訓練法，所精心編輯而成的。您只要花五分鐘，就能記住一種實況，且在短時間內融會貫通，靈活運用。

本書最符合現代人的需要，用字淺顯，內容都是日常生活必備的，句子簡短，易懂、易記。例如想請外國朋友吃中飯，該怎麼說呢？本書教您最實用最普遍的講法：*Lunch is on me.*

「**五分鐘學會説英文**」每冊均分為八十課。每課由一句話揭示主題，再以三個不同的會話實況，使您徹底了解使用的場合。三個會話實況以後，列有「**舉一反三**」，包含五組對話，幫助您推展主題的運用範圍。凡是重要的單字、片語，均詳列於每課之後；對於特殊的注意事項和使用方法，則另附有**背景說明**。

錄音帶採用兩遍英文的跟讀練習，隨時可聽可學。

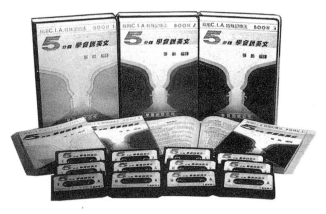

◉書每冊150元，每冊書另有錄音帶四卷500元。

● SITUATION　39 ●

Lunch is on me.

Dialogue 2

A：Miss, may I have the check？
　　小姐，請把帳單給我好嗎？

B：How much do I owe you, Jane？
　　珍，我要付你多少？

A：Nothing. *Lunch is on me.*
　　不必了。中飯我請客。

B：Thank you. Next time lunch is on me. 謝謝你。下回中飯我請。

A：O.K. That's a deal.
　　好的。一言爲定。

B：Let's go. 我們走吧。

〔舉一反三〕

A：This *lunch is on me.* 中飯我請客。

B：Thank you. 謝謝你。

A：Are you buying dinner tonight？
　　今晚晚餐你付帳嗎？

B：Yes. *Dinner is on me.*
　　是的，晚餐我請客。

A：Let's go Dutch. 我們分攤吧。

B：No, *it's my treat*. 不，我請客。

A：*Drinks are on me.* 酒由我請客。

B：What's the occasion？ 要慶祝什麼？

說英文高手

與傳統會話教材有何不同？

1. 我們學了那麼多年的英語會語，爲什麼還不會説？

我們所使用的教材不對。傳統實況會話教材，如去郵局、在機場、看醫生等，勉強背下來，哪有機會使用？不使用就會忘記。等到有一天到了郵局，早就忘了你所學的。

2. 「説英文高手」這本書，和傳統的英語會話教材有何不同？

「説英文高手」這本書，以三句爲一組，任何時候都可以説，可以對外國人説，也可以和中國人説，有時可自言自語説。例如：你幾乎天天都可以説：What a beautiful day it is！It's not too hot. It's not too cold. It's just right. 傳統的英語會話教材，都是以兩個人以上的對話爲主，主角又是你，又是別人，當然記不下來。「説英文高手」的主角就是你，先從你天天可説的話開始。把你要説的話用英文表達出來，所以容易記下來。

3. 爲什麼用「説英文高手」這本書，學了馬上就會説？

書中的教材，學起來有趣，一次説三句，不容易忘記。例如：你有很多機會可以對朋友説：Never give up. Never give in. Never say never.

4. 傳統會話教材目標不明確，一句句學，學了後面，忘了前面，一輩子記不起來。「説英文高手」目標明確，先從一次説三句開始，自我訓練以後，能夠隨時説六句以上，例如：你説的話，別人不相信，傳統會話只教你一句：I'm not kidding. 連這句話你都會忘掉。「説英文高手」教你一次説很多句：

I mean what I say.
I say what I mean.
I really mean it.

I'm not kidding you.
I'm not joking with you.
I'm telling you the truth.

你唸唸看，背這六句是不是比背一句容易呢？能夠一次説六句以上英文，你會有無比興奮的感覺，當説英文變成你的愛好的時候，你的目標就達成。

✌「**説英文高手**」爲劉毅老師最新創作，是學習出版公司轟動全國的暢銷新書。已被多所學校採用爲會話教材。本書適合高中及大學使用，也適合自修。

‖‖‖‖‖‖‖‖‖‖‖ ●學習出版公司門市部● ‖‖‖‖‖‖‖‖‖‖‖‖

台北地區：台北市許昌街 10 號 2 樓 TEL：(02)2331-4060・2331-9209
台中地區：台中市綠川東街 32 號 8 樓 23 室
　　　　　TEL：(04)2223-2838

‖‖‖‖‖‖‖‖‖‖‖‖‖‖‖‖‖‖‖‖‖‖‖‖‖‖‖‖‖‖‖‖‖‖‖

ALL　TALKS ②

編　　著 / 陳 怡 平
發　行　所 / 學習出版有限公司　　　　　☎ (02) 2704-5525
郵 撥 帳 號 / 0512727-2 學習出版社帳戶
登 記 證 / 局版台業 2179 號
印　刷　所 / 紅藍彩藝印刷股份有限公司
台 北 門 市 / 台北市許昌街 10 號 2 F　　　☎ (02) 2331-4060・2331-9209
台 中 門 市 / 台中市綠川東街 32 號 8 F 23 室　　☎ (04) 2223-2838
台灣總經銷 / 紅螞蟻圖書有限公司　　　　☎ (02) 2799-9490・2657-0132
美國總經銷 / Evergreen　Book　Store　　☎ (818) 2813622

售價：新台幣一百八十元正
2002 年 1 月 1 日一版四刷

ISBN 957-519-302-4

第二册 學習內容一覽表

LESSON	CONVERSATION	TYPICAL PHRASE	ACTIVITY	EXERCISE
1	I Lost My Wallet	遺失物品，欲尋求協助時的實用語句。包括如何用英文描述遺失的物品及緊急事件發生時，如何連絡警察局，救護車等。	兩人一組的活動，看圖練習互相描寫人物的動作。	Complete Dialogues
2	Are You Free This Weekend?	與人定約的實況例句，如詢問是否方便，約定時間、地點、臨時拜訪等實況。	兩人一組的活動，利用提示的句型，相互討論，在應徵的人員當中，爲公司挑選兩名新人。	Complete Dialogues
3	May I Speak to Mr. Davis?	打電話的實用例句，如接聽電話、轉機、留言、佔線等實況。	全班一起參與的活動。練習間接引句（indirect quotation）的句型。	Complete Dialogues
4	I'd Like to Make a Collect Call	打國際電話和長途電話的實況用語。包括接線生的指示、詢問與諮詢服務等。	兩人一組的活動。輪流互相詢問及給予指示。練習教對方如何做某事。	Complete Dialogues
5	I'd Love to Come	練習用英文邀請對方，接受邀請及回絕邀請的實用語。	兩人一組的活動，邀請同伴一同晚餐，相互詢問對方討厭或喜歡的口味。	Complete Dialogues
6	How Nice of You to Come	用英文練習接待賓客的實況用語，從招呼，供應點心，到勸食、送客等過程。	兩人一組的活動。練習爲宴客作計畫，事先用英文將工作分派妥當。	Complete Dialogues
7	Please Turn Right at the Next Corner	搭乘各種交通工具，如公車、火車、地鐵、計程車時的實用例句。	全班一起參與的活動。藉由提示的句型，草擬一份交通路況報導，向全班做實況廣播。	Complete Dialogues
8	How Can I Get to the Station	在路上問路及爲人指示方位的實用語句。練習如何用英文爲老外指點迷津。	兩人一組的活動。利用地圖練習爲對方指路。	Complete Dialogues
9	What Time Is It Now?	練習時刻、日期、年份的表達及頻率的說法。	兩人一組的活動，練習使用often, usually, always等頻率副詞的句型。	Complete Dialogues
10	It's a Beautiful Day	用英文談論天氣的冷熱陰晴，及季節變化等。	兩人一組的活動，利用提示的句型，輪流詢問及回答某地的天氣預報。	Complete Dialogues
11	I'm Going to Europe	在飛機上，海關及住宿飯店的實用語句。	兩人一組的活動，利用what及how的問句對答，完成Smith一家人的渡假行程。	Complete Dialogues
12	Let Me Show You Around	租房子時的常用語句，如約定時間、詢問細節，討論租金等實況。	兩人一組的角色扮演，輪流當房東與房客，練習用英文租一間公寓。	Complete Dialogues
13	I Totally Agree With You	表達同意或反對的實用語句。	活動1：全班一起參與的活動，將全班分成兩隊，進行辯論比賽。 活動2：兩人一組的活動，透過對家族樹（family tree）的問答，熟悉親屬間的稱謂。	Complete Dialogues
14	Review	填充題：複習1-13課的會話（conversation）	角色扮演：三個人一組的活動，複習1-13課所學內容。	

MAP OF TAIPEI CITY

淡水大橋 TANSHUI BRIDGE

圓山大飯店
GRAND HOTEL

淡水河 TANSHUI RIVER

環河北街

延平北路

孔廟

CONFUCIAN TEMPLE

圓山大橋 YUAN

民族西路 MINTSU W. RD.

重慶北路

承德路

中山北路

民

民權西路 MINCHUAN W. RD.

民權東

HUANHO N. ST.

台北大橋

TAIPEI BRIDGE

CHENGTE RD.

CHUNGSHAN N. RD.

YENPING N. RD.

CHUNG CHING N. RD.

民生西路 MINSHENG W. RD.

長巷

南京西路 NANKING W. RD.

長安西路 CHANGAN W. RD.

忠孝大橋
CHUNGHSIAO BRIDGE

中興大橋
CHUNGHSING BRIDGE

環河南街

台北火車站
TAIPEI RAILWAY STATION

中華路

忠孝西路 CHUNG HSIAO W. RD.

林森南路

忠孝

康定路

中華路

重慶南路

CHUNG CHING S. RD.

中山南路

CHUNGSHAN S. RD.

LINSHEN S. RD.

華西街
SNAKE ALLEY

HUANHO S. ST.

KANTING RD.

KUNMING ST.

昆明街

新公園
NEW PARK

中正紀念堂
CKS MEMORIAL HALL

龍山寺

總統府
PRESIDENTIAL OFFICE

LUNGSHAN TEMPLE

華江大橋

萬大路

愛國西路

AIKUO W. RD.

愛國東路 AIKUO E. RD.

HUACHIANG BRIDGE

和平西路 HOPING W. RD.

ROOSEVELT RD.

水源路 SHUIYUAN RD.

莒光路

WANTA RD.

西藏路

HSITSANG RD.

CHUKUANG RD.

歷史博物館
NATIONAL MUSEUM OF HISTORY

香舍里榭大道(Champs-Elysees)和凱旋門

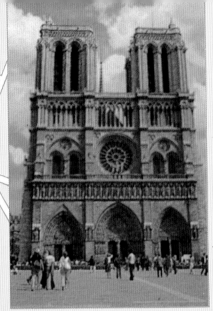

聖母院(Notre-Dame)

凱旋門

香舍里榭大道

羅浮宮(Louvre)
美術館

協合廣場

塞納河(La Seine)

PARIS

羅浮宮美術館

艾菲爾鐵塔
(Eiffel Tower)

聖母院

蒙馬特(Monmartre)
的畫家

子彈列車(TGV)

巴黎大學

香舍里榭大道旁的攤販

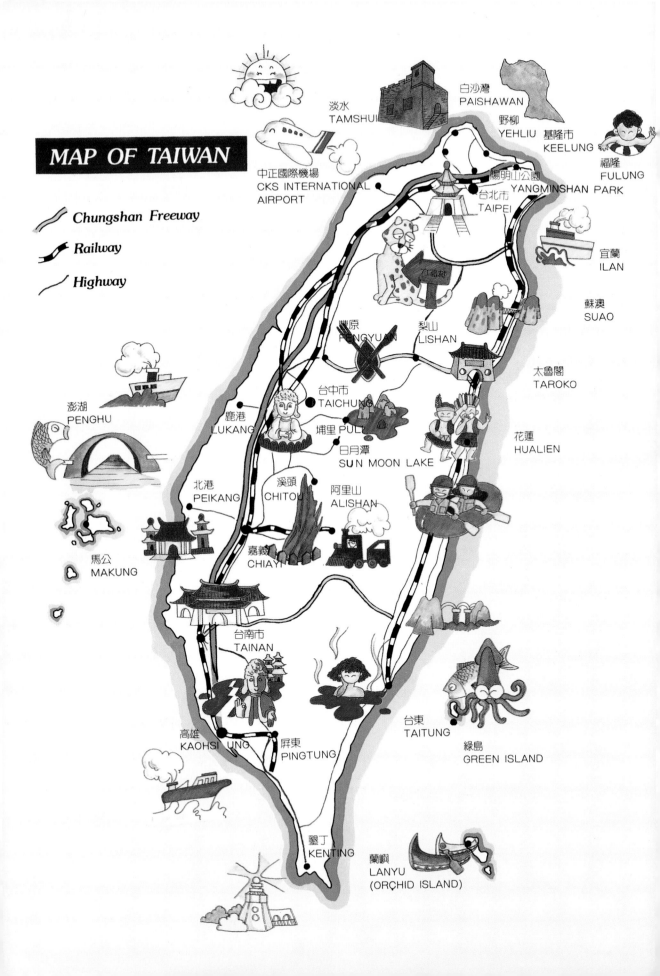

現　　　在	過　　　去	過去分詞	現　　　在	過　　　去	過去分詞
lay	laid	laid	shut	shut	shut
leave	left	left	sing	sang	sung
lend	lent	lent	sink	sank	sunk,
lie	lay	lain			sunken
light	lighted, lit	lighted, lit	sit	sat	sat
lose	lost	lost	sleep	slept	slept
make	made	made	smell	smelt	smelt
mean	meant	meant	speak	spoke	spoken
meet	met	met	spend	spent	spent
mow	mowed	mown	spill	spilt,	spilt,
overcome	overcame	overcome		spilled	spilled
oversleep	overslept	overslept	stand	stood	stood
pay	paid	paid	stay	stayed	stayed
put	put	put	steal	stole	stolen
quit	quitted,	quitted,	strike	struck	struck
	quit	quit	swim	swam	swum
read	read	read	take	took	taken
ride	rode	ridden	teach	taught	taught
ring	rang	rung	tear	tore	torn
rise	rose	risen	tell	told	told
run	ran	run	think	thought	thought
say	said	said	throw	threw	thrown
see	saw	seen	understand	understood	understood
seek	sought	sought	wake	waked,	waked,
sell	sold	sold		woke	woken
send	sent	sent	wear	wore	worn
set	set	set	win	won	won
shake	shook	shaken	withdraw	withdrew	withdrawn
shine	shone	shone	wrap	wrapped,	wrapped,
shoot	shot	shot		wrapt	wrapt
show	showed	shown,	write	wrote	written
		showed			

常 用 不 規 則 動 詞 表

現　　在	過　　去	過去分詞	現　　在	過　　去	過去分詞
awake	awoke	awoke , awaked	drop	dropped , dropt	dropped , dropt
be (am ; is ; are)	was ; were	been	eat	ate	eaten
beat	beat	beaten	fall	fell	fallen
become	became	become	feed	fed	fed
begin	began	begun	feel	felt	felt
bend	bent	bent	fight	fought	fought
bid	bade , bid	bidden , bid	find	found	found
bind	bound	bound	fix	fixed , fixt	fixed , fixt
bite	bit	bitten , bit	flee	fled	fled
bleed	bled	bled	fly	flew	flown
blow	blew	blown	forecast	forecast(ed)	forecast(ed)
break	broke	broken	forget	forgot	forgotten , forgot
bring	brought	brought	forgive	forgave	forgiven
build	built	built	freeze	froze	frozen
burn	burned , burnt	burned , burnt	get	got	got , gotten
			give	gave	given
burst	burst	burst	go	went	gone
buy	bought	bought	grow	grew	grown
catch	caught	caught	hang	hung , hanged	hung , hanged
choose	chose	chosen			
come	came	come	have , has	had	had
cut	cut	cut	hear	heard	heard
deal	dealt	dealt	hide	hid	hidden , hid
dig	dug	dug	hit	hit	hit
do , does	did	done	hold	held	held
draw	drew	drawn	hurt	hurt	hurt
drink	drank	drunk	keep	kept	kept
drive	drove	driven	know	knew	known

第 一 冊 學 習 內 容 一 覽 表

LESSON	CONVERSATION	DIALOGUES	TYPICAL PHRASES	MORE PRACTICE	EXERCISE
1	Meeting People	有關見面問候的對話。	練習打招呼、問候、再見、介紹等實用例句。		Mutiple Choice
2	Talking about the Weather	看圖說出各種天氣狀況	練習表達刮風、下雨冷熱陰晴等例句。	閱讀：Weather Forecast	Weather Forecast in Taiwan（看天氣圖報氣象）
3	Asking Directions	看圖練習為他人指路。	各種表示迷路、問路、指示方向等例句。	練習說明路況	You are here.（問路）
4	At the Western Restaurant	點用西餐的對話。	有關點用主菜三餐、甜點、飲料的實況例句。	① 廣場餐廳的菜單 ② Role Play	Mutiple Choice
5	At the Chinese Restaurant	用英文說出美味的中式食品（燒餅、豆漿…）。	有關吃中式美食及點菜的例句。	中式家常菜名	Mutiple Choice
6	On the Telephone	練習接、打電話的句型。	常用電話英語實況例句。	閱讀：Communication	① Dialogue Reading ② Complete the Dialogues
7	Daily Routines	看圖用英文說出一天的生活流程。（現在式）	練習家居生活的實況例句，包括吃飯、洗澡、做家事等。	① A Bad Day for Teresa（過去式） ② 看圖回答問題（現在進行式） ③ 常用字彙	① 測驗現在進行式的使用 ② Complete the Dialogues
8	The Drugstore	認識美國藥房所賣的東西。	到藥房購物的實用例句。	① 練習使用美國的錢幣 ② 閱讀：The Drugstore in the U.S.A.	測驗數量名詞的說法
9	A Trip to the Supermarket	看圖練習next to、near 等位置表示法。	到超市購物的實用例句。	① 可數名詞 ② 不可數名詞 ③ 常用字彙	① Dialogue Reading ② Match（連連看）
10	In the Airport	練習和機場官員對話。	從劃機位、到登機的實況例句。	① 閱讀：Airport Terminal ② 常用字彙	Complete the Dialogue
11	An Airplane Flight	飛機上的實況對話。	與空服員及乘客交談的實用例句。	① 看圖認識機上設備 ② 練習時間的說法	① Dialogue Reading ② Complete the Dialogues
12	Invitations	練習邀請他人的句型。	邀請他人，接受邀請及謝絕的例句。	遊戲：Invite Your Guests	Complete the Dialogues
13	Western Holidays	互致節日祝賀語的對話。	祝福他人及回謝對方的實用例句。	① 閱讀：Western Holidays ② 歌曲：Silent Night Oh, Christmas Tree	Word Puzzle
14	Chinese Holidays	互致節日祝賀語的對話。	談論有關中國節日的實況例句。	① 有關中國三大節日的語彙 ② 閱讀：Chinese Holidays（元宵節、端午節、中秋節）	Mutiple Choice

英語看圖即席演講

主　　　編 / 劉　毅

發　行　所 / 學習出版有限公司　　　☎ (02) 2704-5525

郵 撥 帳 號 / 05127272 學習出版社帳戶

登　記　證 / 局版台業 2179 號

印　刷　所 / 文聯彩色印刷有限公司

台 北 門 市 / 台北市許昌街 10 號 2 F　　☎ (02) 2331-4060

台灣總經銷 / 紅螞蟻圖書有限公司　　　☎ (02) 2795-3656

美國總經銷 / Evergreen Book Store　　☎ (818) 2813622

本公司網址　www.learnbook.com.tw

電 子 郵 件　learnbook@learnbook.com.tw

書＋MP3 一片售價：新台幣二百八十元正

2014 年 9 月 1 日新修訂

4713269380863

Improvised Speeches from Pictures

▶ 「萬用開場白」及「萬用結尾語」是本書最精采的部分。20篇英語即席演講,以「一口氣英語」的方式,三句一組,九句一段,容易背,加快速度,變成直覺,就終生不會忘記,唯有不忘記,才能累積。熟背的演講,說起來有信心。

書+MP3一片280元

LEARNING PUBLISHING CO., LTD.

00280

4713269380863